AN EYE FOR AN EYE

When the light went out Mimi slipped the knife out of its binding, clenching the handle as Doc moved to the cot. She aimed at his lower stomach and drove the blade upward as hard as she could. He yelled and fell back. She stabbed again, her hatred of him rising to choke her.

Doc fell to the floor, jabbering and blubbering, begging for mercy. Mimi turned on the light and grinned down at him, lying there clutching his stomach with his bloody hands. She sneered, spat in his face and walked out.

Now her mind was clear again and she knew what she had to do.

I'll get the rest of them—Spud, Rocky, Dopey—one by one. I'll maim them, make them crawl. That's the only way I'll ever be whole again—the only way I'll ever wipe out the memory of their rape . . .

AUTHOR'S PROFILE

A mid-Westerner by birth, Stuart Friedman has seen most of America in his numerous travels and now lives in Indianapolis.

Among the various activities that have occupied his time are selling advertising, working with a foundry maintenance gang, selling real estate and the operation of a labor-industry counseling service.

He turned to writing as a career in 1938 and his first published book was a well-received history of Indiana. He has written many stories and articles for leading national magazines, and his books include the recent Monarch bestsellers NIKKI, THE FLY GIRLS and RASPUTIN: THE MAD MONK.

A Compelling Novel

RAVAGED

Stuart Friedman

Author of RASPUTIN: THE MAD MONK

WILDSIDE PRESS

RAVAGED

Cover Painting by Ray Johnson

✤ ONE ✤

MIMI DANFORTH HAD NEVER lived in such a tough neighborhood and it always upset her to pass those hoodlums ganged up outside the candy store. If she went out of her way to the next Avenue she could get home without passing them. She *could* let low scum dictate what public sidewalks she could use, she thought as she finished putting a 25-lb. block of ice in her wagon with the groceries. but she wouldn't!

She pushed back her shoulder length hair and stood up, a brown-eyed blonde girl in loose-fitting blue jeans and short-sleeved white shirt that almost hid the womanly blossomings of her slight young body. There was a defiant, lip-thrusting scowl on her softly pretty oval face as she headed down the Avenue. As she neared her street Mimi's quick stride shortened, her thin legs moving like snipping shears so close together that her bobby socks grazed at the points of her ankle bones.

She turned the corner and there they were. Four or five of the nasty-mouthed, ducktailed bunch were slouching around and jiggling to some rock and roll from a transistor. Mimi told herself there was nothing to be scared of in the daytime, nonetheless she got that tight, breathless feeling.

They called themselves The Rustlers. They wore tight black denims and "hangrope" belts with metal snakehead buckles; star-shaped "sheriff badge" patches were sewn to the seats of their pants. Others came down the street.

One pair, T-shirted in the warm Indian Summer weather, cut diagonally through an after-school stickball game; three more, trailed by rowdy little boys, swaggered over a hopscotch layout in the middle of the broad walk, laughing at the outraged screams of several little girls.

5

The Rustlers and their Rustlerettes, who wore black denims two sizes too small, sometimes "took a walk." They'd fill the whole sidewalk, forcing people against parked cars, cellarway railings or up onto the tenement stoops. When one of the Rustlers came home after an arrest or stretch in reform school, his Rustlerette sewed another sheriff badge on his pants seat. Since they had found out her name and where she lived, Mimi dreaded them.

They spotted her and their faces, whether thick or narrow or pimply, took on the same leering, jeering expression.

"Man, dig Little Red Riding Hood. Hey, baby, come to Granny!" Dutch, the beefy blond, called. He wolf-howled. "A-a-r-r-oow!"

Spud, the tall skinny one with the big Adam's apple, stopped jiggling to the rock and roll long enough to howl: "A-a-r-roow!"

Dopey, the giggler, giggled, then howled: "A-a-r-roow . . . woo!"

Mimi moved along the curb edge of the walk trying to ignore them.

"Dutch, Ole Pard," the pimply, pasty-faced Rocky drawled, "yore plumb loco. It ain't Little Red Riding Hood. That's Little Hot Pants going to sit on a cake of ice. Hello, Mimi. Hello-ee Meemee!"

When Doc, the blue-eyed handsome one who looked so clean cut, bowed toward her, Mimi turned her face. Doc spoke in a deceptively soothing voice.

"Howdy, Miss Danforth, ma'am. Don't pay no mind to these imperlite hoss thieves. You'n' me'll just mosey up to your pad and. . . ."

When he said that word she gave him a brief, scornful look, then went on while the others snickered, hooted and yelped.

"Is she *old* enough?"

"She's fifteen. Is she *big* enough?"

"If they're big enough they're old enough. If they're old enough they're big enough."

She twisted her face toward them.

"Shut up, you stupid fools! You're disgusting. Now, you lay off of me! Just lay off!"

Mimi rushed on while they mimicked her in falsetto

voices. She wished she'd never seen this loathsome street. If only her father hadn't died . . . if only she was back on their old clean, quiet street in their lovely house! Her eyes filmed and she swallowed painfully.

A blast of rock and roll struck her so suddenly that her whole body jerked. She spun, her eyes frantic, and hit out at the transistor which the lanky Spud had thrust, full-volume, at her head. He retreated in mock terror.

She turned back to her wagon. One front wheel had gone off the curb and the block of ice tilted against the side of a car. When she tried to yank the wagon up by the handle, the ice threatened to fall. She braced her saddle shoes apart, bent forward and lifted the whole wagon. Conscious that the seat of her jeans had drawn snug and that the watching Rustlers might pat or pinch her, Mimi glanced nervously across her shoulder. The wagon toppled. In a minute three of them were forcing their help on her and smirking.

She grabbed the wagon handle and almost ran with the wagon. She looked back and they were strolling along after her. At her stoop they caught up.

"Pardners, how can a little ole gal like that there get that there stuff up to the fourth floor?"

"She can't. We'll take it up. Mimi, you run up and unlock your pad."

"You leave me be!"

There was a woman rocking a sunning baby in a carriage on the next stoop. Mimi looked pleadingly at her.

"Go on you bums, leave her be," the woman threatened. "I'll call the cops."

The three Rustlers laughed and walked on down the street. Mimi got the wagon into the building, rolled it back to the dark end of the hall. She was so nervous her hands were shaking. Before lifting the wagon into the dumbwaiter she got her breath. She kept peering at the front entrance door. She opened the dumbwaiter and hoisted the wagon onto it. She hurried up to the fourth floor.

She opened the door of the dumbwaiter shaft and pulled down on the rope but it didn't budge. She tilted her upper body forward across the sill and peered down the shaft. Dirty tenants sometimes threw down their garbage and junk; it landed on the roof of the dumbwaiter carriage, jamming the ropes or adding so much weight that it was a strain to pull it up.

Even if she could find the janitor he'd be nasty and slow about doing anything and the ice would melt too much. She frowned. She couldn't quite make out if the top of the carriage was clear. Although she could easily pull the extra load down and unload it in the cellar, she was scared to. Besides, her mother had *absolutely* forbidden her to ever go down there alone. Reaching up and grasping the rope with both hands she tugged hard. The rope moved and she smiled. She watched the dumbwaiter rise, enjoying the rhythm of her swift, easy, hand-over-hand motion on the rope.

Not till the carriage was almost up to her floor did she sense that it was coming *too* easily. Through the ropehole in the top she saw another pair of hands moving on the rope in time with hers. She gasped, grabbed confusedly for the down rope then tried to slam the shaft door. But the dumbwaiter rose above the sill, and a long, skeleton-like face with over-bright eyes grinned at her.

It was Spud! One of his long arms shot out toward her. Mimi leaped back. With her eyes riveted unblinkingly on him she began to run backward in swift halfsteps, a hand reaching sidewards, touching the stairwell railing.

Spud was unfolding his lanky frame from the boxlike enclosure. He was out and running along the hall when she reached the newel post at the bottom of the stairs leading up to the fifth floor. She went up two steps at a time, her legs driving, her hands on the rail pulling. She glanced back to see him coming up like a falling scarecrow. She rushed blindly to the next up-flight of stairs. It led to the roof.

She was halfway up when he caught one of her shoes. She fell painfully onto the point of her knee, righted herself, kicked out of the shoe.

He made another grab and his fingers got a hold on her jeans, clawing in under the waistband. She was only five steps from the top where a solid steel door opened onto the roof. She kicked and lurched and, grabbing the steel rail uprights, tried to pull herself free of him. He let go her jeans, got a grip on her bobby-socked foot.

She heard a *snick,* felt a needle jab her heel. She twisted to look back down her body at him. She saw the gleaming knifeblade, its point poised on her heel. His almost skel-etally thin face was flushed; his small recessed eyes were bright with excitement. Mimi stared at him, moistened her lips and said as calmly as possible:

"That hurts! Stop it! You're not going to get any place with me that way. Or any other way!"

"You gonna be good or do you want to see what Spud can really do with a knife?"

"Show off for your Rustlerettes! If you think rough stuff impresses *me,* you're crazy! Now let me go and get out of here!"

He released her foot, renewed his hold on the waistband of her jeans and moved himself up several steps. He was panting slightly; strands of long hair fell greasily over one eye; he kept swallowing, rolling his big Adam's apple up and down his throat. He put the side of the knife blade against her upper cheek, and his long face pushed close to hers. He grinned.

"Scared?"

She was frozen. Speechless.

"You know what I could do, Mimi?" He moved the knife blade slightly on her cheek. "I could take a pinch hold of them purty, curly eyelashes and pull your eyelid out away from your eye and slide the knife up in there. Then if you didn't kiss me nice I could just cut your eye-lid wide open. . . . You going to kiss me?"

She covered her eyes with both hands and started to scream at the top of her voice. He mashed his hand against her open mouth. Instinctively she bit. He pinched her nostrils shut, and kept his hand on her mouth so she couldn't breathe. She began to struggle in terror.

"Promise not to yell if I let you breathe?" he demanded in a low, hoarse voice.

She nodded vigorously. He let her have a breath or two, then suffocated her again. Spots of blackness came floating and swirling across her vision. She was shaky and intimi-dated when he let her breathe freely. He stood her up, held her around the waist from behind and began to move his hand over her hips. He probed into her pocket, got her apartment key.

"Give it back! You got to! Give it back! I *got* to have my *key!*"

He jingled the key out of her reach and started down

the stairs. Mimi spun and pitched upward toward the roof door. Below, she could hear the chuffing-hissing sound of Spud's voiceless laughter. The steel hook was tight; she brought her fist up under it and it flew open. She bumped the door open with her shoulder and hip and almost fell onto the roof.

"Woops!" Dutch caught her.

He, Doc, Rocky, Dopey and another Rustler she'd never seen, swarmed over her and crowded her back into the building. They'd reached the roof through another building. There was a cunning about their not entering this one openly and about Spud's tactics that added up terrifyingly to a prearranged plan.

Two of them darted ahead down the stairs. Flanking her, two others held her by the upper arms, half-lifting her. Somebody clutching a fistful of her hair from behind pulled her head back, stretching her smooth young throat into a rounded arch, defenselessly exposed. He kept muttering threats to cut her throat. They hurried her down, their footsteps a rushed tumbling. Mimi stared up at the frostglass skylight windows with a helpless, falling sensation, her breath held, her fingers and toes clenching.

In the fifth floor hall her hope flared wildly. Somebody . . . . she could hear the radio . . . . WAS home up here, after all. The one pulling her hair didn't have his knife out. He'd been using his free hand on the stair railing. She filled her lungs to scream. Her glance flicked to the right rear apartment door. Dutch and another Rustler were hulked there at the closed door, ready to block off and bully anybody who got nosey.

On her floor the only one home was Mr. Jossepaki, so old and wheezy he couldn't even help himself.

The hold on her hair loosened and she got her head up. Her apartment door was open and she could see Spud inside. Both window blinds were down and yellowish light, with sky blue threads showing through the cracks, filled the box-like room. Her scarred upright piano, the purple and yellow bathmats on the raw-looking, deep-cracked floor, the greenish broken-spring armchair and lamp, the pink-flowered covering on the second-hand daybed sofa, looked dismal. But it was home.

"Get out of there!" she shrilled furiously at Spud. At the same time she swung herself forward, spreading her

10

legs and ramming her feet against the door frame. "I *won't* go in there with you!"

She was roughly silenced and rushed inside. She heard the door shut and lock. Then she was standing surrounded in the middle of the room, wobbling a little, her knees trembling, her breathing very quick.

Spud, Doc and Dutch, standing with thumbs hooked under their rope belts, formed a half circle in front of her. Their breathing moved the metal snakehead buckles so that each green glass eye and red glass tongue gave off tiny flashes. Behind her, somebody switched a transistor on low, and Dopey said:

"What a cheesy dump!"

Mimi spun around, flaring: "Get out. All you dirty trash get out." She turned full circle. "Everybody!"

"Don't yell!" Dutch, the strong-looking thickset blond, put his fist close to her face. Jerking her head back she pushed his fist away.

"I won't yell. If you get out. Now." She pushed back at her hair, looked from face to face with jumpy eyes. "All of you. For the last time I'm going to *tell* you the same thing I've been *showing* you. I don't play around! I don't walk sexy! I don't dress sexy! I act careful; mind my own business. I never once flirted or invited you to bother me. But I can't go down that street without getting insulted. I *had* to put up with *that*. So I did. But not this pushing me around and threatening me, and breaking into my home!"

They didn't touch her while she talked, except once she had to push a hand away from the seat of her jeans. Mostly they just ran their eyes up and down her body and exchanged private grins.

"You ought to be arrested for what you've already done, but all right. Forget that. But if you don't leave *now* I'll scream, as loud and long as I can. Even if you beat me up. I'll tell the police!" Her voice faltered. Her cheeks were flushed with anxious excitement.

"I'd think," Mimi rushed on, a sudden note of pleading desperation about her voice, "anybody who was proud of being tough would be ashamed not to stand on his own two feet like a man. Instead of ganging up and bullying. Besides, if *I* was a boy I'd have more self-respect than to bother with a girl who didn't want me."

She tilted her chin up haughtily. She realized that the

11

attitude was such flimsy bravado as to appear ridiculous. Suddenly her eyes betrayed her, welling hotly, so that she had to blink rapidly. Even so, tears slid onto her cheeks so that she had to wipe frantically.

"Boo hoo, boo hoo!" Dopey said behind her and giggled.

Spud was gazing down at her hip and leg like a grinning hawk and Mimi realized that, unconsciously, she'd been swaying from side to side. She tensed her thigh muscles, stopped the motion. She cleared her throat and drew a full breath, and the lift of her chest defined her small firm, conical breasts. Dutch, who'd been gazing at her shirt-front, blinked and grinned widely, nudging Doc. Mimi hunched her shoulders, pulled her shirt forward and looked at Doc.

She had been directing most of her appeal to Doc whose handsome, clean-cut look made him seem less a stranger. It was as if he came from her world and knew her and didn't really belong with these others. And he was looking at her face, not her body. Looking up into his nice blue eyes she saw kindness. When he smiled Mimi knew he was on *her* side! The fright warmed from her wide brown eyes, her delicately curved, pink fresh mouth relaxed.

"Doc, you understand. Please tell them for me," she said in her high clear voice.

"The kid's not ready," Doc said. He petted her cheek, then ran his fingers back into her wavy light brown hair, as if he valued and appreciated her. "She's tender. Too young and too pretty to rough up. Wait'll she's a woman."

"She is already!"

"Oh, no!" Doc protested. "I'll show you! She's got no chest!"

He'd been rapidly unbuttoning her shirt. He pulled it wide open and skinned it back off her shoulders. He grinned down at her with lips drawn tight to his teeth. Hands were pulling down the top of her slip, fingers unhooked her bra. She backed into a wall of bodies; hands pinched her bottom. She tried to get her thin arms up over her breasts.

"Why," Doc said in mock wonder. "I was all wrong!"

When she was stripped down to the waist they held her securely and handled her bare, pink-tipped breasts. When she submitted, they hurt the tender flesh, when she struggled so that her breasts moved agitatedly they guffawed

12

and cheered as if she was putting on a show for them. Enraged, she kicked, tried to claw, and screamed:

"Damn you! DAMN you!"

The transistor was turned up louder. Seconds later a wad of rough towel was rammed into her mouth. She felt the zipper opening on the hip of her jeans. She crossed her ankles, locking her legs together, clenching her buttocks. She'd been staring glassily at the ceiling, her head with the gag in her mouth held by somebody behind her. She squeezed her eyes shut as if somehow that would cover her as they pulled off the jeans, her panties and even her bobby socks.

There was an impact about the naked beauty of her body. Her skin glowed like rich pink-tinted white satin and she was exquisitely formed. Her feet arched slenderly, her legs tapered gracefully, the rising flare lines of her sleek thighs merged smoothly with the feminine softness of her hips and tight, round buttocks. The incurve at the small of her back was sharply defined, her upper body rose, widening slightly from the pleasing narrowness of her waist; her shoulders sloped gently. Her body was in a process of growth, elongating and filling out; this inner surging and the radiance of clean, vital flesh gave an indefinable glow to her whole being.

They whistled, giggled and howled. They stroked and felt and pinched and rubbed themselves against her nakedness.

"A virgin! Take the Doc's word."

"Take the Doc's word, hell! By God! He's right!"

"Damned if he ain't! Aaar—ooow!"

She squirmed and lurched and couldn't free her arms. Her voice was swallowed by the towel. When she kicked at them her inner thighs were exposed. They touched her privately, relentlessly, till she was dancing with outrage. Worse, her quiveringly alive flesh was terribly sensitive and sometimes one of the more cunning ones touched her in a way that caused exciting sensations and made her hate herself and sob heartbrokenly.

Then she was being pulled by the wrists and pushed and slapped toward where she would die before would go. She tried to collapse the wrists. She yanked her left hand free of Dopey and clawed out at Rocky's eyes. He flinched and half-relaxed his grip on her wrist and she got that arm

13

free. She fell joltingly to the floor, hitting with her upper back and head.

One of them tried to pull her up by the hair; she clawed his wrists bloody. The pair who held her ankles tightened their grips, twisted her foot punishingly and dragged her. She hooked her arms in under her knees and using all her strength she drew her knees to her chest, then drove both legs forward with all her force, hitting one of them so hard he struck the wall. She got both legs free and kicked, her knees and feet driving, striking. At the same time she clawed out blindly, her fingernails gouging whenever any of them got near.

Then she was pinioned again, lifted bodily. They set her briefly on her feet and somebody put his forearm under her crotch, raising her till her toes were above the floor. Crowding and bumping clumsily they struggled her into her bedroom. Somebody hit the side of her head so hard her senses spun.

Then she was being tumbled off-balance onto the thin mattress of her own squeaky bed. She was on her back, holding her eyes shut, her legs tightly crossed. Hands mashed her lurching shoulders down. Other hands encircled her ankles, pulling them apart.

She couldn't keep her legs locked. She flopped onto one hip, rolled wildly onto the other. She freed one leg and kicked somebody so hard he swore and twisted her foot almost off the ankle bone. The wrenching pain almost made her scream. She thought she would faint; she wanted to. But every fiber in her was rawly alert.

She felt someone between her knees. Then she was touched privately. She began not to breathe. She held her breath thinking she would hold it till she went blue and fainted and died. But she failed. She found herself gasping for air and shivering with terror as it started to happen. Her chest began to heave with dry sobs; spasms ran through the muscles of her stomach; her legs jerked.

The intimate pressure increased steadily, painfully. It became suddenly violent and she felt a tearing and a raw, scalding pain. In panic she thought her very vitals were being ripped by some terrible animal, like a maddened rat in her flesh. She could no more keep her eyes shut than she could stop breathing.

She saw the face above hers, tense and ugly with vicious

14

triumph, like an insane distortion of Doc's handsome face
. . . . hours later it was Spud's twisted animal features,
weeks later . . . grunting Dutch . . . then pimply Rocky
. . . she tried to retch, but there was Dopey, ungiggling
and vile . . . the one she'd never seen had a lip scar and
his mouth twitched like a face in a nightmare. . . .

Then there was nobody. She stayed uncovered, unpro-
testing, broken. A low, growling voice was saying in her
ear:

"If you open your mouth to your old lady, we'll get
you. We'll bust in here and cut your throat. Hers too.
Hear me? Tell ANYBODY and we'll KILL you. Hear
me?"

"Yes," she whispered.

"Understand me?"

"Won't tell," she mumbled. "Won't tell. Don't hurt me
any more. Won't tell . . . stop . . . don't . . . please
. . . won't tell . . ."

"Quit blubbering Talk so I can hear you!"

She had to repeat. To promise. To swear. Then he was
leaving.

She watched his back and moved her lips saying silently:
"I hate you . . . hate you . . . hate . . . hate."

✣ TWO ✣

WHEN SHE DIDN'T MOVE she didn't hurt. Mimi lay torpidly while her senses slowed down. A heaviness as comfortable as winter blankets settled over her body. Once, a long, long time ago when she'd had a bad cold her mother had sat on the edge of her bed stroking ointment on her chest and crooning to her in a gentle voice.

Now the words and melody glided through Mimi's mind. She could almost feel the slow caressing of her mother's fingers, the penetrating warmth of the ointment. Quiet light filtering through a blue silk lampshade had glossed her mother's dark hair and lovely, heart-shaped face. "Sweet and low . . . sweet and low . . . wind of the Western sea. . . ." she had sung. On the "w's" her beautiful lips shaped a kiss and each time they did Mimi touched them lightly with her fingertips. Enjoying it, her mother had sung the words several times. And all the while they had gazed lovingly into each other's eyes.

The feeling between her and her mother had been absolutely true. Then, subtly, a little insincerity crept in as they played up the scene for Mimi's father, watching from a nearby chair. A quiet steady man, he loved them deeply but couldn't express affection easily and valued it all the more between his girls. His elegantly tall, fullbreasted Diane, with her very fair skin, glossy dark hair, vivid sky-blue eyes and ravishing smile, didn't always provide such peaceful scenes.

Usually her mother was easy to be around because she was warm and gay, pleased with herself and all the world. She liked praise and pretty things and she coaxed instead of scolded, turning on the charm and blarney that got around everybody.

But she could be stormy and her boiling point was un-

16

fixed. She'd be indifferent to plagues that would drive calm women frantic; at other times the slightest sass from Mimi brought on a shouting, door-slamming dish-smashing tantrum. Afterwards she'd be extra-loving and sorry. Sometimes she'd have what Mimi's father called a "silent explosion" when she suffered inwardly until the sadness in those bright eyes was unbearable to see. It would tear her father apart.

He would bring her out of it and she would begin to reproach herself bitterly because she was a bad wife and mother (untrue), extravagant and emotionally immature (true).

Mimi had often eavesdropped, listening with a sort of uncomfortable astonishment, because at these times her mother was like a child, and her husband, patiently answering, explaining, criticizing, scolding, was like her father. For weeks afterward her mother would be at her best.

Then she'd go on a shopping splurge, knowing it would make Mimi's father mad.

Once, parading before a department store mirror in a luscious negligee she looked at the price tag, rolled her eyes and told the salesgirl: "I'll take it." To Mimi she'd confided, "Pat's going to raise the roof about this one!"

He did. The negligee, some haremish underthings, nightgowns and four out of six pairs of frivolously pretty shoes went back to the stores.

Her mother didn't get mad, either. In fact, Mimi learned as she grew older, her mother not only didn't resent it, she liked his assertion of authority.

Other men were always flirting with her mother, and she responded . . . . up to a point. One time her father broke his hand on a man's jaw at a New Year's party, but usually it didn't come to a fight. Her mother would keep going a little farther all the time, but as if she was looking across her shoulder to see that her Pat was watching and would stop her before she got in trouble.

She was a good cook, but she loved specialty dishes and routine meals sometimes bored her. Once Mimi remembered her father coming in tired from work to find both of them dressed to go out.

He stopped and frowned and said, "No, we're not going out."

"Now, Pat, don't grump. It'll do us all good. Be sweet."

Her mother had given him a lingering kiss and a lot of blarney. Mimi had started to make over him, too.

He stomped away from them both. He turned around and shook his finger at Mimi.

"That's a habit of your mother's you're not going to pick up, Mimi. All this use of sweet words and general female wiles! Dinner out won't be enough, you'll start badgering me to go to a movie afterwards. Right, Mimi? No, don't look at her for a cue!"

"Well," Mimi hesitated. "It would be nice to see a movie."

"Have you done your homework?"

"Yes."

"Now Mimi. Have you?"

"No, but Daddy, I could get up early. Besides, the teacher likes me and . . ."

"You could get by with not doing it? And you'd be willing to do so, willing to exploit and misuse your teacher's liking for and confidence in you!"

"She studies hard, Pat. She's a conscientious kid. Maybe this once? She'd like it."

"No, she'll not. If she's conscientious, she'll not. What's the truth in you say, Mimi? Would you enjoy the picture when you knew that it was distracting you from your real purpose and additionally causing you to betray the good faith of your teacher? No. The subject is closed. And now, princesses, I'll be proud to take you dining."

And proud was the word. He always made them know he felt that way when he was in public with them, together or on a walk alone with her or having an evening on the town with her mother. At parties he didn't take the second drink and watched her mother to see that she didn't sneak too many or flirt too much. People said he was as dull as his profession, statistician, but they didn't understand. He was serious. He disciplined their lives and however much they sometimes wanted to defy him they appreciated the way he held things together.

After he died two years ago everything went to pieces. When it got dark in the evening her mother got nervous and said the house was spooky. They'd go out to eat and maybe to a show, then afterward have a treat, just to delay going home. The loss of sleep told on Mimi and one day

18

she stayed out of school. When she woke around noon her mother was hovering over her.

"Poor baby, do you feel all right?"

"I guess."

"What would you like for breakfast?"

"I don't know till I wash my face."

"Of course. So what I'll make you is a surprise breakfast."

She had a headache and wasn't hungry but her mother had taken such pains and was so anxious to please her that Mimi ate with a show of enthusiasm.

Afterward, her mother sat across from her in the nook and lit a cigarette.

"I cried all morning, but the way you put away that food gives me confidence. I'll confess something. Yesterday afternoon I went out in the garage and started looking through the little west window fifteen minutes before you were due home from school. Then you turned that corner with Linda Vance and Sassy Thompson and my heart just jumped. They're nice, bright, properly raised girls and I compared you with them and, Mimi, I was so happy I just can't describe it.

"I thought a hundred things. How you've got no more hips than a boy and how you're stretching out, and the *marv*'lous way you walk, not trying to be sexy at all and still so feminine and nice and charming. Your face in that hood was like a solemn little flower." She reached over, took Mimi's hand and held onto it tightly, and her eyes filled. "I told myself," she said chokily, "I told myself I loved you so much that I couldn't be anything but a good mother. . . . Then *look* what happened," she suddenly wailed. "Keeping you out late again and hurting your health and ruining your education! I'm such a bad mother!"

"You're not either!"

Mimi got up hurriedly, went over and sat beside her and hugged her.

"I'm rotten!"

"That's not so!"

"Are you sure, Mimi?" She gazed steadily at her.

Mimi looked at her worriedly. Her slender heart-shaped face was so drawn that her fine, high cheekbones stood out a little. Her light blue eyes, so beautiful with their fringe of

19

curling black lashes, looked so innocent and helpless that Mimi had to fight to keep from crying.

"Of course I'm sure, Mommy!" she said in a rush. "Haven't I been in a hundred homes and seen all the mothers? A lot of their children wish they had you. Almost every girl I know has wished lots of times she had a different mother. I never even *once* had that wish," she assured her. Beside her leg, Mimi crossed her fingers. Her mother's hand came down there, touched her hand. She laughed suddenly.

"You sweet little liar!" She took Mimi's face in her hands and kissed her cheeks, forehead and nose. "Well, anyway most of the time you like me. And honey face, I really enjoy having the full responsibility for you. It works double; it'll give me strength and confidence. Pet, get my purse from the hall table."

When Mimi returned she watched her mother fix her face, frowning into the pocket mirror so absorbedly that Mimi grinned. She liked seeing her pleased with herself and confident. Her mother lit a cigarette, waved the match out airily.

"The company your Daddy worked for offered me a job. I can hold it! Don't you think so?"

"Yes."

"You don't sound very sure . . . well, I'm not either, but. . . ." She frowned slightly, drew a deep breath. "You'd have to come home to this empty house. I'd worry. Every minute. Unless your girl friends could come home with you on some days and you could go to their houses on others?"

"We could do that. But I'd miss you. I'd miss you awfully. Anyway till I got used to it."

"Then you'd get used to it and NOT miss me. Oh, I just can't *stand* it."

"Please, Mommy, Please don't get emotional. If you do, I will. And there's nobody unemotional to stop us."

"You're right! Mimi, you've got his good sense. He raised you right. It was different with me; *my* father didn't give one damn. Even if he had of he didn't have any brains to bring anybody up. . . . Well, I CAN hold down a job. Starting next week. If you're sure *you* can take it."

"I'll be able to. And I can help out by baby sitting. And

we can save on my music. I don't have any desire any more to be a pianist anyway."

"You're not going to take up a lot of time baby sitting or quit your piano lessons or any such thing. There's a few thousand insurance and some bonds and with what I make we can live all right. What we're going to both do is just like your Daddy was always saying. Work toward becoming our best selves. We can make a clean fresh start right this minute and go forward with our lives just like he wants us to."

For awhile her mother held the job and also took a typing-shorthand course, so that they had a sense of going forward. Her mother became a swift typist, but couldn't spell. At the end of the school semester she quit the job because she believed they were treating her like a charity case. She put the house up for sale and they moved to Pennsylvania, where her mother's family lived.

It wasn't the right move. As soon as the house was sold they got away. First they had a vacation at a Florida luxury hotel. It cost too much. Her mother began seeing men. One of them took over her investment problems and vanished with nearly every cent they had.

Mimi's mother had always enjoyed a few drinks, but after her husband died she swore off, afraid that on her own she couldn't control it. After they'd lost the money and returned to New York to live in successively cheaper furnished apartments, Mimi's mother began again. It seemed that one or two drinks knocked her out. Then Mimi caught on that she'd sneaked several drinks before taking any in front of her.

Her mother got all sorts of jobs . . . . clerking, filing, assembly work in small factories. Sometimes she was laid off; other times she got fired. Just as often she became offended at something and quit, announcing later to Mimi in a defensive-aggressive way, that the job had been beneath here. After all, she was Mrs. Patrick Danforth, a quality person with pride and position and meaning. At first she rarely let Mimi know she was drinking. When they moved into a cheaper neighborhood and began to lose spirit, she drank oftener and openly.

Men came and went. She was always searching for a proper father for Mimi, and some of them had been not

as good as her Daddy, but of the same decent type.
Though Mimi didn't want a father, she wanted her mother
to have a man smart enough and strong enough to lean on.

But during the several weeks they had lived here on this
terrible street her mother had taken up with trash, one
after another. She would invite them out for a "family
type" meal and pretend that she thought they were husband possibilities, looking for a wife and home.

What they were looking for was one thing. After they
had enough drinks they got it. In her mother's bedroom.
More than once the man would still be there when Mimi
got up next morning. Some handled her mother intimately
right in front of Mimi.

One really horrible one had even leered at Mimi and
sneaked pinches and feels when her mother's back was
turned. Mimi had been afraid to upset her mother by saying anything. In some moods she might even side against
her. Once, when a nice one had walked out after a fight,
Mimi's mother had turned on her.

"I could get a husband like *that*. But who wants anybody else's brat into the bargain?"

She'd been sorry almost at once, but it was the truth.

Even when there wasn't a man and drinking her mother
often came home tired out and discouraged. She'd light
into Mimi, criticizing everything she did or ever had done.
Afterward, of course, she'd be sorry and they'd get emotional and make up and cling together. Only last week
they'd reminded each other that it was never too late, that
they would start all over and come up to their best selves
from that moment on. . .

Now Mimi lay inert, her young body mass-raped, her
spirit violated, and tried feebly to believe it was still true
that a fresh start was always possible. She couldn't.

"Mommy, please come, please come home," she whispered. A yearning sadness filled her breast and tears slid
out of the corners of her eyes down her temples. "Please
hurry!" She sighed exhaustedly.

Sleep, sweet sleep, sweet healing sleep. Her eyelids
closed heavily. They opened at once. She stared at the
cracked ceiling of the dingy little room, remembering the
growled threat to kill her if she told her mother or anybody. She squirmed miserably. The motion sent pain like

raw flame through her; her head and eyes ached splittingly.

She tried to sit up and fell back. The strain quickened her heartbeat, intensified the pain. She lay utterly motionless. She would sleep and try to wake before her mother got home. In case her mother *did* get home and saw her jeans and slip and panties flung around the front room, then saw her naked here, she'd just say . . . she'd just say she was a slut and had had a party. Except . . . her mouth quivered . . . her mother would never believe it. Besides, the bed must be a mess, sickening with filth and blood.

Mimi knew that if her mother came in on such a sight after all she'd been through the blow would break her. Her heart. Her will. Her pride.

It wasn't whether she could get up, she HAD to. She sat up, then stood up, moving very slowly. In the bathroom she cleansed herself and ministered to her injuries as gently as possible. But she kept wincing and sometimes the pain was so acute she had to stop and just hold on.

She put on a housedress and clean bobby socks and went groggily into the front room. She stepped into one saddle shoe, and started out of the apartment thinking the other was on the stairs. But it was by the armchair. Her door key, she saw with relief, was on the piano keys.

She picked up her jeans, felt through them for the $2.47 change from the five her mother had given her that morning. She went through the pockets a second time, felt in the shirt. She raised both blinds and, squinting, searched the floor, daybed and chair. Blinking nervously she went out of the apartment to hunt, going clear up to the roof door. She came back empty-handed. She remembered folding the bills around the coins in the grocery after holding out money for the ice . . . the ice! She hurried to the dumbwaiter, which was still at her floor but empty.

She went down to the first floor, her gaze scouring every square inch of stair treads, hall floors. Her wagon wasn't at the dumbwaiter. Spud must have entered this building at the rear of the cellar and taken her wagon off down there. With a resigned sigh she went to the cellar which smelled of garbage cans, ashes and dampness.

The floor was uneven, the dim, narrow passage lined

with storage rooms where winos, drunks and worse some-times lurked. She was glad to hear the scrape and clank of the janitor's shovel in the coal bin and at the boiler and more glad to see her wagon, even though a quarter of the ice had melted and the grocery sack was in a puddle and soggy.

By the time she got upstairs, put the ice in the box, the groceries on shelves and sinkboard it was a quarter past five. She had an hour till her mother got home and two hours of things to do. She did the worst first, wadding up her ruined bedspread and hiding it in the back of her closet. She replaced it with a quilt.

She opened the tall, narrow airshaft window, then went to the front room. to do the next worst thing: pick up her torn-off clothes. She moved with a skittery speed, her thin arms darting, snatching, retracting, and it didn't take long. Wrapping her hair in a scarf and getting the broom, dust-pan and dust rags made her feel housewifely. To save time, she told herself, she could neglect parts of her usual routine. Only she couldn't. Like a compulsion she went through every detail and in the exact sequence; the only difference was that she cut out the lingerings.

She'd written a poem for English class last year and copied it in her diary. It had said that beauty was some-where to be found in everything; to search it out and ap-preciate it gentled the senses; and that one could store these riches and they would be an impenetrable armor against ugliness. At this time of day the lowering sun had raised the shadow line across the buildings on the side of the street to her floor. The sunlight on the ceiling and upper walls gave the room a clean, airy luminosity and there was a beauty about it. Mimi gazed at it and with no emotion at all said something she couldn't imagine herself saying.

"It's a goddamned lie. A goddamned lie!"

More and more people were getting home from work. She heard them on the stairs, and talking, walking around, shouting, playing radios and TV in the apartment above, below, back of theirs, across the hall. She stood frowning, peeling the potatoes too fast. She got them on to boil, opened the can of green beans, set them on the stove with-out lighting the gas burner yet. She set the table, washed her breakfast dishes. She carefully hacked out two pieces

24

of ice, put them in glasses which she left by the ice in the box. They'd be all ready to pop the Fizz-Fruit tablets into for the drink she and her mother always had the minute she got home.

She put on a clean housedress. She combed her hair, avoiding as much as possible looking directly into her own eyes in the medicine chest mirror. She washed her face again, put on a teensy bit of lipstick, then rushed into her mother's bedroom, went through her own drawer in the bureau and selected a polka-dot ribbon for her hair.

Her mother not only didn't like to come home and find her sloppy looking but she wanted a bright mood and affection. The last would be easy. Mimi would be so glad to see her she'd just swarm her with hugs and kisses. At ten past six she turned the gas on low under the beans, set the hamburger out beside the skillet, ready for her mother to cook and put the margarine on the table.

She went to the front room, raised the window and leaned out across the sill, hoping to see her coming. Not yet. Mimi stood in the middle of the room with a sudden terrible sense of confusion. She started to twist her fingers, darted back to the bathroom, put on hand lotion. She came back, rubbing in the lotion and stood staring at the piano.

The Hanon book of exercises was open on the rack. Her hands started to shake as she sat down. She had good hands. Her teacher, Professor Ceccini, complained that her bass was weak and her melodic lines weren't crisp and brisk enough, but he admitted she had fine hands. Still a little too narrow, but her fingers were strong, their octave and one note reach was excellent. She worked hard and Professor Ceccini said there was a musician in her in spite of flaws in her technique. And her technique *was* improving. A little. She spread her hands and looked at the clusters of musical notes and her eyes filmed over. But she knew these exercises by heart.

She started the runs, four octaves up and four octaves down. She barely noticed the six out of tune strings because something else was wrong. Instead of rolling, rushing rhythm, the runs had the sound of frenzy. Too fast. Slowing, her fingers jumbled. She rubbed her hands on her knees and started again, her shoulders tensing. It was worse. She sat motionless. Her face began to squeeze up like a rubber ball. In a second she was crying, holding her hands over her face, her elbows striking discords on the keyboard.

She rushed to the bathroom, sloshed her face in cold water. She caught up a towel, flung it aside with a little yelp. It was the one they'd gagged her with. She used another, applied powder carefully. She went and looked out the window and her mother was coming up onto the stoop directly below.

She didn't look up before entering the building. She wore a short beige coat with artificial violets on the lapel and a matching beret with a twig of stiff purple cloth rising jauntily from the center. Seen from that angle, with her head lowered and her thin shoulders drooped, her mother looked sad and small. Maybe she was just tired or disappointed because Mimi hadn't been watching from the window for her. Or . . . Mimi hugged herself, her eyes stark . . . maybe she'd lost her job again.

✣ THREE ✣

MIMI WAITED FIRST at the open door, then at the top of their flight of stairs. Finally, when she heard her mother reach the floor below and start along the hall, she went three-quarters of the way down. Mimi stood grasping the rail and grinning at her from the steps, thinking that trouble had really made her prettier. Her heart-shaped face was more slender and there were hollows like faint shadow stripes down her cheeks, accenting her fine, high cheekbones. She wore bangs in a charming, careless pattern of dark curves alternating with the smooth white skin of her forehead.

For two or three steps she kept her gaze down, her mouth lightly compressed as if sulking and she pretended not to be aware of Mimi . . . but she couldn't help grinning. She lifted her face toward Mimi, opening her eyes wide. They were the bluest blue eyes with the blackest black curly thick lashes, and her smile was like an angel's. It was unimaginable that she could ever get mad, and in fact she couldn't stay that way or let anybody else. When she'd come out of a temper and turn on that sweet smile you couldn't help melting. Sight of it now made Mimi grin wider, then make giggly-gurgly sounds of pleasure.

"Hi, precious."

"Hi, Mommy."

They embraced briefly. Mimi fell in alongside her and they climbed the steps with arms around each other's waists.

"You make the silliest sounds, Mimi. A good thing, too, after not watching for me."

"I saw you sulking like a big baby; then you got ashamed of yourself, didn't you?"

27

Her mother laughed. When they entered the apartment Mimi wrapped herself around her, hugging tightly. Presently her mother's arms closed around her, holding her close.

"Oh, Mother, I'm so glad you're home."

"You don't know how good it is to see you, too, pet!"

They separated, and her mother went toward her bedroom, taking off the beret, fluffing her hair and saying:

"I'll freshen up. Get the ink ready to drink."

"It's not either ink."

In the kitchen Mimi took the glasses with ice in them out of the icebox and filled them with water. When her mother came in and put on an apron, Mimi dropped in the raspberry-flavored seltzer disks and watched them geysering, dancing and staining the water purple.

"You get a kick out of that, don't you?" her mother said affectionately.

"M'm h'm." Mimi handed her one glass.

"Here's to us."

They touched glasses and drank. As always, her mother made a face; as expected, Mimi laughed and protested.

"You know very well it's delicious."

"If *you* like perfumed ink, *I* like perfumed ink. You just sit down at the table while I finish the cooking. You've got almost everything done. That's fine, it's such a help, Mimi."

"I wouldn't even try to make the meat and come up to your gravy. Did you have a pretty good day?"

"Oh, well, you know. School all right? You didn't have any trouble with those bullies in the halls, I hope, or those tough girls in the rest room?" She peered at her, casually questioning at first. Then, one eye narrowed. "What was it?"

"Nothing."

She came over to the table, put a finger under Mimi's chin and peered into her eyes.

"Listen, Mimi, your mother's thirty-two years old. It's time already she's grown up." She tapped her own chest lightly. "I admit for awhile it was me leaning on you, but I'm over that. You've got a right to look to me for protection, not the other way around. Don't spare me. Something happened. One of those hoodlums that they ought to kick out of the schools gave you a bad time. Right?"

"N-no."

28

"Mimi. Honey. Listen. It's bad on my job. Yes. I've got that old premonition that a pink slip's about due. True. The work's beneath me. The people I've got to associate with are aggravating. I get tired and discouraged. Still and all, nothing could really make me give up as quick as feeling that you're pulling away from me, not trusting me, not confiding. I can take it. I want to. I want to know I'm responsible for you and carrying your troubles along with you. We never were in this bad shape before, we know it. But we know too that it binds us closer together than ever. You wouldn't hold anything back because you think I don't *care,* it's not *that.* You're trying to make it *easier* for me. Only it doesn't."

"Well, in the washroom, two of the girls said some things and laughed at me."

"That all?"

"Yes."

"It's because you've got nice manners and quality that they don't like you. You know what that amounts to, when low people resent you? A tribute. Your Daddy always said that. Remember?"

"Yes. And you know what? I already feel *much* better. I'll remember to be like you. *Above* things. Proud, like you. I tell you, Mother, there's not one woman in a million that could have managed the way you have on your own."

It pleased her mother so much she had trouble keeping a dignified face and when she went back to the stove she nearly swaggered. She just loved being told she was strong and above things because they both knew she was really weak and that everything overwhelmed her.

Finishing the meal her mother leaned back and lit a cigarette and watched Mimi sprinkle sugar on a margarined slice of bread.

"Honey, I told you to get a cupcake or piece of fruit for yourself. Bread and margarine and sugar's no kind of dessert."

"Bread and *butter* and sugar."

"Ha! If you'd been brought up on the stinking stuff like I was you'd never mistake it for butter. Saturday I'm doing the shopping and one item is a stick of the real stuff. Incidentally, how much change have you got from the five?"

"There was $2.47."

"A dollar-fifty for your music lesson leaves 97¢. Two

days till my pay; I've got subway fares but no coffee break money. Give me the odd forty-seven cents. You can have the other half-dollar for cokes or candy or whatever. That'd be plenty for two days even if we were rolling. I figured out what I'll do if I get runs in these stockings." She laughed. "Cut off my legs."

She put out her cigarette, started gathering up their dishes.

"While I'm clearing the table will you get my black, kickpleat wool skirt, honey? I've got to press it. And I'll do a couple of your blouses while I'm at it."

"Mother."

She looked at Mimi, waited.

"I lost it. The money."

"Oh, no! You *didn't*. You crazy kid. *Honestly,* Mimi!"

"I couldn't help it. I tried to find it. I went back and looked everywhere. I just feel *terrible* about it."

"You feel terrible. You know what I had to do to draw that measly five in advance? *Crawl.* Answer questions about what I do with all the wealth they lavish on me in that rat trap. I practically had to sign an oath I wouldn't blow it all in on caviar and champagne and ocean cruises in my yacht. Where'd you lose it? Where'd you first not know you had it? Hell, you know what I mean. Where? We'll go look together. The way your eyes are always in the stars, maybe you didn't know things might fall *down?"*

"In the building here. When I came in I felt my pocket and there it was."

"Which pocket?"

"My pants, then I put it in my shirt."

Her mother sat scowling into space, then snapped her fingers.

"That's it. You leaned into the dumbwaiter shaft and it fell down somewhere. I'll find the damned thing. . . ." She started out of the room.

"But I looked everywhere," Mimi cried, "even down the cellar."

Her mother came back and stood over her with fists rammed on her hips.

"You went down that cellar against my orders?"

"Yes, but only *because!"* She pleaded. "Won't you understand? I didn't *mean* to lose that money, Mommy."

"Well, my God, I know you didn't mean to. You think

I'm yelling at you because I think this is a Sunday School and you've been a bad girl? You think it's a twiddly little moral issue? Forget it. As far as intentions go, you're as snowy-white-Jesus-little-lamby as ever. Only, for God's sake, Mimi, we're living real life now, and intentions don't matter the first damn. What matters is the money! Now, don't look down in your lap and mash your mouth together that way like I'm being abusive and mean to you. . . . You *hear* me? Look up in my face! That's it, but don't you dare stare that way like I'm something horrible.

"I won't be looked at that way, like I'm an ogre. You have no belief in me, have you? No. Because we've come down to this dump. You see surfaces. You know everybody treats me with contempt, so you do, too. You take their judgment. It was fine when we were well off and I was treated big; you too respected me because everybody did. But alone, you don't judge with your heart. No, not with your heart."

She stopped suddenly, her back to the room, and clutched the edge of the sink. "You don't deny it," she said hollowly. "You sit and listen to me getting hysterical and saying things I don't mean and you don't move or say a word or try to help me *stop.*"

Mimi just sat, staring dully, her hand resting upturned on her lap, her shoulders slumped.

Her mother spun around, her face wild.

"DO something!" she screamed. She clutched her upper stomach. "I can't stop myself!"

"I can't stop you," Mimi said tiredly.

Her mother streaked past her out of the kitchen, into the big bedroom and slammed the door. In a few minutes she came back. She petted Mimi's shoulder.

"Sorry, pet. Let's try to get on the upswing. I'll make us some strong, hot, black, vile coffee. Okay?"

"All right."

When it had been brewed, Mimi sipped hers and immediately made a face. "It really *is* vile."

"Isn't it though! But it puts gristle in your guts."

"That's right."

"Anybody that can drink this coffee can take anything. This is all temporary. I've got this big feeling of confidence about our futures. And Mimi, we ought to try to remember the details of this kind of life. When we're past it and

31

among the pampered kind of people who couldn't have survived it, we can talk about it amusingly. Snoot 'em, in a way, with all *we've* experienced." She lit a cigarette and said in a too casually gay voice: "And tonight you're not to get upset about Mac, because it's the last time I'll be seeing him."

"Mac?" Mimi alerted unpleasantly.

"You remember him. Mac Keeling. He was here a couple of times."

"I remember," Mimi said bitterly. He was the worst of them; the one who'd leered at her and felt her intimately when her mother wasn't looking.

"I admit he's unrefined, but underneath his crude manner he's not so bad."

Mimi snorted.

"He didn't have advantages as a kid, I can tell that much. His home life was messed up worse than mine. Granted, he drinks too much and doesn't watch his language, and out of a clumsy natural affection he takes liberties with me which I know you don't like any more than I do. He's a physical type, but he works hard and they like him in the warehouse. He's held one job four years and makes good money, so you can see he's stable."

"He looks like that's where he lives. In a stable."

"I'll say this. He's more generous than a lot of educated people I know. It's not bad having a friend to borrow a few dollars from in case . . . well, I won't throw it up to you that you accidentally lost some money. But try to be a little understanding of me. I'm a woman as well as a mother."

"A woman needs a man, not an animal. I hate him, Mother, I tell you. I want to claw him and hit him when he touches you. It's like mud being splashed on something very high. It's wrong. Even if you were a stranger, it would make me sick to see a coarse thing like him handling anyone fine and beautiful. He's so far beneath you it's horrible."

"He knows I'm too good for him. I suppose that's his appeal for me. Compared to him I feel like real quality again."

"You can get mad if you want to, Mother, but you aren't real quality when you're with him. You go down to his level, that's what you do. The first drink you don't. The second drink you don't. The third drink you do."

"You count?"

"Yes. And you become just plain disgusting the way you wiggle and giggle and simper and let him kiss you."

"I do?"

"You know very well you do. I just think I'm having a nightmare and it can't be you. I just feel like sinking through the ground. And when you see me looking unhappy and critical you say things to me that . . . well . . ." she drew a painful breath, dropped her gaze.

"What? I just tease you. Nothing awful."

"Oh, no? Oh NO? You say I'm a police force. An old woman at fifteen. Stuffy. You're not proud. You don't like me. I know you're drunk and try not to pay any attention. But it hurts my *feelings*." Her eyes blinked rapidly, feeling hot with tears. "You'd think THEY were your own instead of me."

"But you *know* different. Well, I'll not drink so much . . . and you needn't be around him. You don't even have to say hello. Just stay in your room. I won't have him here again."

"Tell him I'm sick and he can't come in tonight!"

"Please, darling. I won't let you be upset. You needn't even know, but I've *got* to . . . well . . . I promised him he could come. This time."

"I'll hear you in your bedroom," Mimi said in a low voice. "And I'll know. I know why you've *got* to have him. Well, I know one thing. I am *never* going to have any sexual desires. Never, as long as I live. If there was some way to be operated on so that I'd never have any feeling that would make me want to be dirtied, I'd have it."

"Well, you'd be lucky. I'm not that lucky. I do have desires. Strong ones. I can't HELP it. I wouldn't want to be a creature who COULD help it, for that matter. Oh, what am I supposed to do, Mimi? You're so smart, so unaffected. Is all you can think of is that I should try to be a nun or something? Dry up all the natural juices in me?"

There was a long silence, an avoidance of each other's eyes.

"I'm tired," Mimi said at last. "And I want you, Mother. Please, I want you. I want you to come in my room and tuck me in bed and sit with me, because I'm so sad. I'm so SAD. . . ."

She got up and went into her bedroom. She got into pajamas and slipped under the covers, feeling chilly and feverish at the same time. Her head ached. Her heart ached. Finally, her mother came in and sat in the dark and talked to her. She stroked Mimi's face, kissed her and promised not to have Mac in.

Suddenly, when she was on the verge of sleep Mimi couldn't hold it in any longer. She was going to tell what the Rustlers had done to her. She drew her mother's face down close and whispered into her ear.

"I've got something to tell you, Mommy. When I was coming back from the grocery. . . ."

"What are you saying, pet? I didn't hear."

"They. . . . up here in our apartment. . . . right on this bed!"

"Darling, you're half asleep. I can't make out a word."

"I was thinking about you, loving you, Mother, needing you . . . I wouldn't do anything to hurt you . . . Good night. . . . Good night!"

She drifted off to sleep. She didn't know what time it was when she woke.

She didn't know what woke her. She had an obscure, fleeting impression of hearing something in the last instant of sleep. Something abrupt. Violent. A heavy thud or slammed door. She eased her head up from the pillow to listen with both ears, her neck tense. Dim mechanical voices from somebody's TV drifted in the airshaft.

There was almost no other noise in the buliding. It must be late. A motion overhead caught her eye. Her open, airshaft window was swinging slightly on its hinges. She realized the noise that had waked her had been the window banging against the bedroom wall. The outside wind didn't dip down this far into the shaft unless it was very strong, which it wasn't. But if her bedroom door opened a rushing draft might come through the window and bang it against the wall. Her back was to the room, she couldn't see the door at the foot of her bed.

Suddenly the wall a few inches ahead of her glowed faintly with yellowish light that vanished almost at once. She smelled cigarette smoke.

34

"Is that you, Mother?" she said in her mind. Her lips and throat were too husk-dry to speak or even whisper.

Her mother always looked in on her before going to sleep. Often she stayed awhile, sitting on the edge of the bed, petting her a little and kissing her before leaving. Mimi remembered now that she had been here much earlier. Mimi had got up to go to the bathroom and take two aspirins and her mother had come out of her bedroom into this one. She'd petted and kissed her and tried to breathe away from her because she'd been drinking. Mimi was uncovered now but she distinctly remembered her mother covering her.

When her mother had gone Mimi had hurt as badly as just after she had been raped, and she had made a kind of compress of the covers, wadding and pressing them tightly and soothingly against her crotch. She lay on her side now, the covers clamped between her thighs, her supple body forming a closing circle, her upper back and shoulders curving toward her drawn-up knees. It wasn't her mother in this room. When she'd had a few drinks she slept like the dead. She'd never have got up and come in a second time!

It was *the Rustlers* who had come back!

She couldn't move and she couldn't cry out. For an instant she was glad. That's how a nightmare was. That proved this wasn't real. Six Rustlers couldn't stand that quietly. Just one of them might have come back. There was a chainlock. He couldn't have got in the front. Or this window.

Her mother had been drinking. That meant Mac *had* come into the apartment.

A floorboard squeaked behind her. Her breath hung.

The wall glowed faintly again as he dragged on his cigarette. Mimi felt a chill like ice-cold breath on her spine. Her pajama jacket had hiked up baring several inches of her smooth young back. The thin cloth of her pajama pants was stretched taut, revealing the contours of her bottom nakedly.

He touched her there! The feel of his vile, stroking fingers was like shock. She gasped.

She flopped on her back and rolled frenziedly onto her right side, her left arm streaking out like a whiplash to

35

the lamp on her tiny study table. She knocked it over, then seized its metal shaft and pulled the lamp onto the bed and turned on the switch.

"Get out," she hissed, her soft little face stiff with fright. "Get out! Get out!"

Caught in the light, Mac grunted and scowled, his low forehead furrowing tightly. His massive, short-fingered hand pawed out at the lamp. Mimi jerked it out of reach and in a sitting position she scooted herself back toward the window corner of the bed, holding the massed covers like a shield in front of her. Mac seized the covers and yanked so hard that Mimi came forward with them for a foot before she could let go. Her teeth began to chatter.

Mac coughed and wheezed and came crawling onto the bed toward her, looming like an ugly, mindless giant with his blob ears, wide squashed nose, thick, unshaven chin. He was undressed down to his underwear and hair like black worms crawled out of the undershirt and a powerful sweaty odor came from his body and his breath smelled of whisky and bad teeth.

She whimpered and slapped out futilely, then in a defensive gesture she lifted the lamp and hit him. It yanked the cord plug loose, throwing the room into terrifying darkness.

The buttons flew from her pajama jacket as he caught the top and ripped downward. She tried to stand up, and he pulled the jacket top clear off. He clutched her soft little breasts in his coarse paws. Her nails gouged at the backs of his hands and she tried awkwardly to stand up. Her hip scraped on the window sill, then she was half-sitting on it, hitting and kicking at him, her breath swift and shallow, her vision swirling dizzily.

He was trying to pull down her pants. He pulled the waistband below her navel. She pulled up, he tugged harder, half baring her hips. She got herself covered with a violent motion that made her lose her balance. She started to topple backward into the airshaft well, a horrible thirty-foot drop.

Involuntarily she grabbed at him. He lifted her bodily on one arm. His other hand got the pants off. She clung with both hands to the window sill. She started to scream. He hit her arm and broke her grip on the window and dragged her violently back onto the bed.

36

"Shut up, you! Just shut up!" he ordered. He was snuffling his nose and breathing noisily.

She screamed at the top of her lungs, throwing her head back and shutting her eyes. He hit at her with his fist, grazing her head. He started to curse her and tried to strangle her. He got both hands on her windpipe and straddled her, clamping her twisting, pitching body with his knees. Her screaming gagged and choked out. Blindly she kicked and struck with her fists at any part of him she could. His hold released on her throat and she started to scream piercingly again.

The door banged open. Her mother reeled in, holding something in her upraised arm, and began to hit him and yell and curse and beat his head and back.

He didn't feel the blows. Insane with lust, he stayed on the bed. His body began to lower toward Mimi.

Then her mother did something he felt. He bawled with pain and hurled himself to the floor and sat holding himself. Her mother began to beat his head again. Enraged, he lumbered up after her mother. Mimi could see them in the hall light. She rushed out with the lamp and hit him savagely and repeatedly from behind.

Her mother ran to the kitchen and came back with the bread knife. She held it in both hands overhead and she leaped at him, plunging the knife at his body. He jumped aside and ran. He threw the front room armchair in front of her and got to the door and out. Her mother followed him into the hall and down several steps, stabbing wildly at him time and again, her face murderous and white as death. Her mother came back in, yelling to Mimi.

"Open the front window!"

Her mother rushed to her own bedroom, came back with his clothes and hurled them out the window.

They watched and he stepped out, picked up the pants, went back in the building.

Grim and silent, her mother went to the kitchen, came back with some milk bottles, a whisky bottle.

Her mother leaned over the sill waiting, watching with glittering eyes, her face drawn. When he stepped out again, she hurled a bottle that smashed inches from him. Her mother waited intently while he went into the building with his shoes and shirt.

37

"If I can knock him out I can get down there and stab him, the son of a bitch!"

When he came out she took careful aim. She missed and swore. She hurled another as he went down the street at a run.

She took up the whisky bottle, sighted, then lowered it, looked at it speculatively. It wasn't empty.

"He's too far. No use wasting good whisky. I'll kill him tomorrow. I swear to God. Put on the chain lock. I'll get your robe and slippers, you poor baby. I got there in time, didn't I? Tell me. I did, didn't I?"

"Yes. Yes."

"Poor kid. You're shaking like a leaf."

"You too, Mommy. Please, relax."

Her mother vanished, returned with Mimi's robe and get your robe and slippers, you poor baby. I got there in the kitchen, carrying the whisky.

"This time I earned a snort."

"You sure did."

"You, too. This once. Medicine." She carefully poured drinks in tumblers, watered Mimi's and thrust it at her. "Down the hatch."

Mimi drank it all. It tasted gaggingly horrible. But she kept it down and soon it began to warm her. She grinned.

"It's good."

"That's my baby." She drank her own. "Hey, wasn't I a riot?"

"Whew! You were *marv*'lous!"

"Sure I was. That's all we've got to keep in mind. We're both marv'lous. Want another little one?"

"A *big* one!" Mimi laughed.

✤ FOUR ✤

THURSDAY SHE DIDN'T go to school. First off she got the bedspread out of the closet where it lay like a hidden fester and put it in an outside trash carton. Rid of the last remnant of the rape Mimi was confident she'd begin feeling better right away. But she didn't push herself.

Listless and physically tired out she slept most of the day, on the sofa or curled in the front room armchair. Repeatedly she attended herself with the medicated solution in the bathroom. She ran a tepid bath and fell asleep in the tub. She rallied before her mother got home so she wouldn't send for a doctor who might discover everything.

In bed that night she was brittle with tension. She tried to reason with herself and remember pleasant things like that trip the summer she was seven. The car had hummed along the western highways and sometimes even her father felt like singing. Easing off, she remembered Disneyland and the taste of hot biscuits and fried chicken and the look one morning from the balcony of their motel of the turquoise-colored water in the four-leaf clover shaped swimming pool and the cake layers of colored rocks down in the Grand Canyon and the soaring feel of staring down into that gorge. She relaxed and dozed and suddenly the top of the Grand Canyon where they were standing began to slide and she woke with a lurch.

One after another she concentrated on remembering good things. Her swollen sense of richness and virtue when she was hurrying home with a good report card; her solemn joy when she and Mildred Dale had vowed eternal love and friendship when they were nine, her sense, time and again, of being floated along on certain utterly beauti-

39

ful passages of music. In each case she would feel a bliss-fulness, then slowly, dismally, the feeling would turn to fright and ugliness.

She got up and stood in the dark, shivering. She was more profoundly afraid then when Spud and Doc and Rocky and Dopey and Dutch and the twitching-scar-lipped Rustler and Mac had been attacking her. Something in her had clung throughout the physical horror to the certainty that if it was ever over it would be done forever. Cleansed of the filth of their touch her body would heal itself as any bruise or cut did and somehow her real self would not be affected.

But it *wasn't* over. The things she cherished deep in her mind and spirit were being raped too. Those creatures had even reached back into the clean, sweet safe part of her life to spoil it, twisting beauty into ugliness, pleasure into pain. Now she didn't have any confidence in what she *had* been. If it kept happening and every small nice thing she'd ever known was attacked what would she have left?

It couldn't happen, it *couldn't* happen that her whole past good life could be killed! If it was killed she would be somebody else; the real person she was wouldn't exist. She would only be just what her body had been, a used thing, powerless, belonging to low, horrible creatures. She herself would be a horrible creature . . .

What if they forced her to be a Rustlerette, to do what-ever they wanted whenever they wanted her to and made her listen to their talk till she talked that way too, and *thought* their way and scorned any girl who was innocent?

If they made her steal like they did and drink beer and go to their "blowouts" where the girls competed to see which of them could dance the dirtiest? If they made her listen to their kind of music all the time till it was the only kind that ever went through her mind? They could beat her up and scare her every time she tried to break away. She would become somebody she hated!

She stood there barefoot in her pajamas, one knee jogging nervously against the edge of the bed and suddenly she was somebody else seeing herself. Seeing the whole scene. Herself naked on her back on the bed being raped, and she could see the expression on her face. The look of pain and despair that twisted her face was *ugly*. The raw

40

vision of herself made her drop to her knees at the edge of her bed.

She folded her hands together and started to pray, as when she'd been very small. She had been ugly even then because she'd known her Daddy and Mother were watching and listening and instead of *really* praying she'd been saying what, and looking the way, they liked. In those prayers she had always *not* mentioned the *wrong* things she had done, just saying nice-sounding things. Oh, God, what a dishonest and hypocritical thing she'd been, even then. She remembered how specially gooey sweet she'd be to her mother if she had stolen a cookie or pretended not to hear when she'd been called.

In a sudden burst she knew that what made her bad wasn't the rape; that had just pulled back the curtain and exposed the truth of what she'd been hiding all her life. In addition to being a liar and a thief and a hypocrite and sacrilegious in her show-offy prayers she hadn't even been pure sexually. She had been sneaky.

One time, right when she was being kissed good night her hands under the covers had been where they shouldn't be. There had been those times with Ruthie Day; peeking in the bathroom at Ruthie's big brother, then she and Ruthie had looked at each other and hid together in closets and giggled and played. Once she'd whispered to a boy in kindergarten a word that she didn't even know she knew and he'd told teacher and . . . and . . . Even since she'd been old and had breasts she had dishonest ways of not exactly touching herself wrong but enjoying frictions and pressures and . . . and . . . *thoughts.* . . .

Had she been careful enough not to make herself tempting? Hadn't she let her hair show? Didn't she always keep clean and pretty instead of being sloppy and dirty and unattractive, and so wasn't she really partly guilty of that rape? No. No! But now she was ashamed! She didn't know how she could ever walk down the street or go to school or let anybody see her. Her loathsomeness would be sensed. No one ever again would think of her as a sweet girl or gentle or innocent or worthy. . . .

She stayed out of school Friday, too, telling herself she'd be all right by Monday. In the early afternoon she forced herself to take a walk in the fresh air. Dozens of women were outside, gossiping, sunning their babies,

41

watching their pre-schoolers. When some of those she knew by sight nodded or smiled Mimi responded, but she was too edgy to stop, as she often did, to look at any of the babies.

Little kids banged cans, howled and shouted at the tops of their voices; a bull-voiced man at a third floor window and a knife-voiced woman on the walk carried on a conversation; a roaring-whining-rumbling-gear-clashing truck came along behind her; from ahead the torrent of sounds from avenue traffic funneled into the street. Sunlight glared from auto windows, blazed like points of broken glass from chrome surfaces. Her ears hurt, her eyeballs felt raw.

Her senses were so painfully acute now that in the past she thought she must have had some kind of shield around her. Like a womb, or great balloon, or invisible membrane. It was as if she had really just come from a womb; even her skin felt extra sensitive and chilly and the ordinary brushing sensation of the light breeze was unpleasant.

The Rustlers weren't around at this time of day but as she came nearer and nearer the candy store she felt weaker and weaker. A terrible heaviness began to settle like fine silt in her body, filling her feet and lower legs and knees and thighs and hips and lower stomach. She was so tired she had to stop. She turned around.

Her heart seemed to be laboring with all its might to push her blood through her arteries, and she thought she was going to pass out. Her face paled and her eyes, suddenly feverishly bright, began to blink rapidly. A band seemed to clamp around her chest and her breathing was quick and shallow and she had a sense of fighting for air. Suddenly she was clammy with sweat as if her whole body had been abruptly squeezed.

Something queer happened to a glaring spot of sunlight on some chrome just ahead. It began to smolder and swirl and a black cloud of smoke rose, expanding quickly to blanket the whole street in darkness. She thought she was having a heart attack and dying. She put out a hand for support on a car roof. She could see herself dead and then she could see her mother seeing her dead. Her mother would go wild and scream and fight to bring her back to life just as she had fought with a knife to save her from a monster, but it would be hopeless and Mimi felt in her own breast her mother's aloneness, her despair. . . . Everything cleared as suddenly as it had blurred and Mimi got back to the apartment as fast as she could.

The minute she was inside with the chain lock secure Mimi went to the piano. Her way of fighting for them both would be her music. Because even if her mother sometimes disliked her music she needed it, needed to know that that best part of Mimi's life was going on. She placed her spread fingers for the first notes of the Hanon runs, the cool touch of the keys under her fingertips inspiring her with confidence.

Years ago she'd written in a notebook in elegant, scroll letters: "Music hath charm to soothe the savage beast." It should have been "breast," not "beast," but either way it was just as true. Her hands remained motionless, soundless on the keys. She got up and pulled down the blinds, then marched herself back to the piano, positioned her hands and fingers on the keys. She remained rigid.

From outside and within the building there were all sorts of sounds. Harsh, chaotic, inferior to the orderly beauty of the music. She knew she must strike out and assert this high thing, this good and strong thing. She couldn't.

She walked around aimlessly, trying not to think about it. She sat and tried to read. She forced the whole problem out of her mind. The moment she returned to the piano she froze . . . like a small furtive animal not daring to announce its presence. She scorned and chided herself and left the room and came back angry. She fairly hurled herself onto the bench as if suddenly she could catch the piano napping. And it worked! She struck all the right notes correctly. The sound swelled, and then hummed diminishingly and finally it died. Because the next notes wouldn't come.

Monday morning she dressed for school, got her books and notebooks into the satchel, and left the apartment the same time her mother did. Mimi was back home in a quarter hour. Tuesday she sat around in a branch library eating candy bars, reading magazines and feeling guilty. Wednesday, a week after the rape, she returned to school.

✤ FIVE ✤

THERE HAD BEEN a cold snap in the weather and she wore
her dark coat and a scarf on her head, carrying her books
in a satchel. Her skirt was schoolgirl drab. Under her
white blouse she'd bound her breasts flat to her chest.
Different streams of schoolbound kids crisscrossed at several corners, heading for public, parochial, elementary,
junior and senior high schools. There were policemen at
several corners and she got safely enveloped in a group
she didn't know and reached the square, dark red brick
building without incident.

There were two Rustlerettes in her home room and
others in some of her classes, but no Rustlers. Those of
the Rustlers still in school were in the upper classes and
except for the halls she didn't have to worry about them.
But the halls, and especially the stairs were very bad.
There were all kinds of other gangs which should have
been some sort of protection since they were each other's
enemies and one bunch might have defended anyone
another gang picked on. But it didn't work that way.
They let each other alone, and smaller kids not in a gang
were like scurrying rabbits and anybody's game.

She glimpsed several bullies in an empty classroom
badgering and probably stealing from a whining, pleading boy no bigger than she was. Mimi hurried past, her
face reddening.

In the locker rooms several separate gangs were hud-
dled. She had to press past one bunch who looked at her
with flat, cold eyes. Down the line two girls stared at her
threateningly; one of them curling up her lip. Nobody was
allowed to wear gang uniforms here, but she knew they

44

were Rustlerettes. Mimi got her coat put away and hurried upstairs.

There were guards stationed in the halls, senior boys and men teachers, including, she saw with a quick smile, her favorite, Mr. Wilks. They watched as much as they could, but they couldn't be everywhere. And things could go on within a moving group; kids surrounded, threatened and hurt and robbed and not daring to open their mouths.

She came around a corner where a fat boy was crawling, crying, and picking up his books. Everybody walked widely around him. Mimi paused and handed him a book. But when he lifted his miserable face to thank her she saw his bloody nose and almost ran from him.

She made her home room and fortunately the big, rangy hard-faced Miss "No Nonsense" Ellenburger was there standing like an eagle watching everybody. Mimi presented the note her mother had written Monday, tried to explain it was mis-dated, but Miss "No Nonsense" just shrugged, not believing anybody about anything anyway.

The first three periods, a Composition Class, a study period, Algebra, were all right. Then to get to Mr. Wilks's class, she had to negotiate two long halls and two flights of stairs. As she started up the last one she saw fragments of white glass on the steps. The landing globe and light had been smashed. There on the dark landing was the twitchy, scar-lipped one and Rocky and Dopey. They stood watching her come up. She turned at once and started to rush back down when a voice from above said:

"It's all right, Miss Danforth. Come on up to class. Now, you punks scatter!"

It was her history teacher and favorite, Mr. Wilks. It was as if he'd been on guard watching out for her from his floor above. He came down toward the grinning Rustlers with an easy, confident grace. When Mimi hesitated he repeated:

"It's all right. When the odds are only three to one with them these punks are never brave. Are you, punks?"

He reached the broad landing and walked right toward them.

"We didn't do nothing, Mr. Wilks," Dopey whined. "Not a thing."

"That's so." Rocky said. "We wouldn't hurt the kid. What're you getting in an uproar about, Mr. Wilks?"

Mimi scurried up around the newel, ran part way up to the next floor. She stopped, turned, and looked down at Mr. Wilks's back. He made a thumbing gesture at Dopey who went alone down the steps. Mr. Wilks stood staring at the other two Rustlers.

One of them said something Mimi couldn't make out. Like lightning, one of Mr. Wilks's fists drove forward right into Rocky's stomach, hitting him so hard his breath whoofed out and his back and head thudded the wall behind him. Mimi's hand went to her mouth and she bit, her eyes bugging as the twitch-lipped one made a sharp quick movement toward Mr. Wilks from the side. But Mr. Wilks saw him and his hand and foot moved at the same time, and the revolting Rustler was tripped, his upper body propelled violently forward so that he had to fling his arms to keep his face from hitting the steps as he fell.

"Now, punks," Mr. Wilks said in a low, carrying voice. "I told you to scatter. You show up in my class tomorrow and I'll throw you out the window. You think I won't or can't? Speak up when I talk to you, weasel."

"Oh, you're big. You can, man. You can. Pick on kids, man, you can. Only maybe outside you're not so big without a whole gang of teachers siding you."

Mr. Wilks turned his back on them and came up the stairs with deliberate slowness. The Rustlers below watched his back murderously for several seconds, then went downstairs.

After they had gone, Mimi let her breath out. When Mr. Wilks reached her she gazed at him for the longest time, her brown round eyes immense and near-worshipful.

"Oh, Mr. Wilks," she said fervently, "You're so courageous. You were wonderful. How can I ever thank you?"

His tightly compressed mouth relaxed in a smile, and his glitteringly angry eyes seemed to calm.

He walked on toward his classroom. She hurried to keep up.

"Thank me by being the kind of student you are. Where've you been, Mimi?"

"Sick."

He glanced at her face. "You *have* been sick. You're pale."

"If you hadn't come along just now I'd have had a relapse. I just can't tell you how much I appreciate it, Mr. Wilks."

"That's all right."

"I'll catch up on my assignments if I have to stay up half the night," she promised.

He laughed. "Mimi, in this class, you'll stay ahead by just staying awake half the *period* . . . here we are."

He opened the door and went in ahead of her, and the minute he came in sight almost all the girls in the class acted stupid. They beamed on him and got coy, and one made a moaning sound of pleasure, and another pretended to collapse in a swoon and one of the jazziest . . . a sexy dark-banged little Rustlerette, wolf-whistled.

Mimi took her seat, disgusted with them and proud of Mr. Wilks's indifference. However much they hung around and showed themselves and flirted and did everything they could to woo him he looked on them like so many pieces of wood.

Right now he paid no attention at all, and said from behind his desk:

"Your assignment touched on the second phase of the French Revolution. Because this whole movement is crucial to our understanding of the key elements in later European politics, we will drop back to the opening phase. I'll re-cap. I advise close attention because a written test," there were groans which he ignored, ". . . covering the material will be given directly after I finish. . . . The monarchial interests in France had been increasingly alienated from the people since the reign of . . ."

Listening to Mr. Wilks, Mimi had to control her impulse to hang onto him with her eyes. She'd discovered during the first week of school that it annoyed him to be stared at fixedly. She kept her gaze moving except during his pauses. Then, when he scanned their faces to judge whether they'd grasped what he'd said it was like a question and she turned her face to him, giving the answer in her expression. Usually, because he made things so clear, she understood and it was wonderful to give him the alert, waiting-for-more look he liked.

Yet, two or three times in the past she failed to understand and her look was cloudy and doubtful and she had felt utterly stupid and unworthy. But he hadn't let her feel

47

that way. He'd gone back to where he'd lost her and lifted her up and brought her forward. She was aware of his pausing now and she knew quite well what he had said and she understood, but suddenly she wanted to be dumb and helpless and she gave him a baffled, supplicating look.

He went over the point, again, supposedly for the benefit of the whole class. But, sitting there behind his desk on the little platform, as on a throne, he focused totally on her. In his case when he looked directly at her it was not only permissible but required to look at him, and she took full advantage of it.

He finished the summary talk and the monitors passed out the mimeographed test questions. Mimi set to work with full concentration. When she finished, she went back over each answer carefully, then carried her paper to his desk. He didn't look up from something he was reading. But when she got back to her seat he was looking at the paper she'd turned in . . . one of the first finished.

She opened her text at the page her missed assignments began.

"The relations between France and England at this time were complicated by" she read, "The relations between France and England at this time were complicated by The relat—"

She sat with her spine curved and scooted forward low in the seat so she could sight him over the top of her book through the thicket of her lowered eyelashes. Until he looked up from her paper and gave his verdict she was non-existent, just waiting to exist, and the feeling had a tight, tingly excitement about it. When at last he looked up Mimi flicked her tongue across her lips and watched intently for his reaction. He was looking directly at her, his face expressionless. Then he partly closed one eyelid in a semi-wink.

It was an act of recognition and fellowship and in it she could feel his warmth and pride in her. It stated the fact that their relationship was on a high, serious level. She restrained her smile instead of letting joy burst childishly all over her face. She sat straighter, opened her notebook and with pen hovering over it she read the text, putting the physical person of Mr. Wilks out of mind.

She did not write Mr. Wilks, Mr. Thomas Radley Wilks, Mr. T. Radley Wilks, Mr. T. R. W., Tom, Thomas, Tom,

Wilks, Wilks, Wilks in her notebook. She did not let her gaze creep up to look at him for several minutes. Then with a quick pang, she wondered if he had left the room. Her glance darted to his desk and the sight of him assured her. It was very hard not to look at Mr. Wilks. Whenever she just had to, she always tried to do it in a way he wouldn't know about or wouldn't be embarrassed by.

Other girls were always trying to seduce him with sly looks or by brushing against him or rolling their hips or flaunting their pointed breasts at him. Mimi didn't want the type of interest she had had in him from almost the first day to be confused in his mind with that sort of thing. It would disappoint him terribly and violate the true, deep bond that existed between them.

He was so high and fine and clean and spiritual that it was almost vulgar to admit how physically attractive he was in that brown sweater, tie and gray jacket. He was taller than average and nicely proportioned and his head was like an art work of heroic sculpture. His handsome face was a strong, masculine triangle standing on the blunted point of his chin, his forehead forming the wide base. There was an elegance about the V line joining his chin and broad cheekbones. Abut his thin, finely shaped mouth there was usually a certain haughty disdainful expression which wasn't at all coarse arrogance but a true knowledge of his own refined superiority. His sharply parted dark brown hair always looked neat. His eyebrows were thick, his dark, well-spaced eyes glowed with intelligence and perception.

He was kind and gentle, even though he had to be tough and mean during the first two weeks of the semester. He had often conducted the class from the rear where he stood directly over boys likely to make trouble.

One day he'd taken a knife away from one of them and he'd actually dragged him out into the hall. Now, any disturbances he got from back there he handled by ridicule because, in spite of his very serious personality he had a sharp wit. When there wasn't trouble he was a dedicated, conscientious teacher. Sometimes when he was trying to make a difficult point absolutely clear to everybody Mimi could detect a pleading in his fine baritone voice. Some teachers hoarded their knowledge but Mr. Wilks offered it as a treasure, almost begging them to accept. This generosity of spirit about him was so sweet that even though Mimi knew almost nothing about his life, she knew one thing, certainly. He was good.

She knew she didn't have a mere, giddy schoolgirl crush on Mr. Wilks. She'd tested herself by imagining what she would feel if he took her in his arms and kissed her. It would disgust her with him. She wouldn't like him at all if he did that . . . he just wouldn't be Mr. Wilks if he became like that.

She lingered after class and approached his desk.

"What is it, Mimi?"

"About my missed assignment. I suppose," she said hesitatingly, "I should just catch up a little at a time."

"That's about it. There's two weeks before any serious exam. You should be up easily by then."

She nodded, started to go, turned back. "Was my test paper all right?"

"Yes," he smiled fleetingly. "Yes. Nearly perfect."

"I learn so easily in this class."

"In your other classes, too, from what I hear."

She beamed at the idea he'd been inquiring about her, discussing her with other teachers. Mr. Wilks was waiting for her to go. She'd noticed before that he wasn't as easy in his manner in person-to-person contacts as he was at a distance before the whole class. She knew she was making him uncomfortable and wanted to free him but she didn't know how to break off. She cleared her throat and smiled.

"You'll be late for your next class," he said, giving her an out.

Instead of taking it she got tangled again.

"It's only a study. Miss Ellenburger doesn't care what you do if you're quiet."

"Mimi, are you afraid to walk through the hall?"

She nodded solemnly.

Mr. Wilks peered beyond her, motioned to someone and called: "Oh, Joe. Joe Banner. . . . Would you mind?"

Joe Banner, a big, good-natured tow-head in a green two-stripe varsity sweater, came up to the desk.

"Yes, sir, Mr. Wilks?"

"You know Mimi Danforth, Joe, I'd like you to see to it that she gets down to—one-hundred-four, isn't it, Mimi?"

"Sure, Mr. Wilks. Hiya, Mimi."

50

"Hello."

"He'll take you down. Don't be frightened."

"All right. Thank you. And you, too, Joe," she said going into the hall with him.

Going down to 104, Joe checked her shirtfront, saw it was flat and didn't look back at her again. At the door of her home room he assured her:

"A little kid like you's got nothing to be scared about. S'long."

"S'long."

It was a relief to hear him say it. She really didn't look like anything more than a board-chest kid now with her breasts bound, so she really needn't be scared.

Still she stayed around on the outside steps after her last period, waiting and watching. At last Mr. Wilks came swinging along. He stopped, put on sunglasses and lit a cigarette. He saw her and exclaimed.

"Mimi! You weren't waiting for me?" He took off the glasses, looked at her.

He wasn't pleased, so she shook her head.

"No."

They smiled at each other and he went on down the steps. She stared wistfully after him. He looked around, caught her looking at him that way and he came slowly back up the steps.

"You *were* waiting for me?"

She smiled, gestured aimlessly.

"Well?" he said patiently, "What did you want? Don't be shy, dear."

"I wondered if I could walk along with you."

He hesitated. "Well, all right. Sure."

"I thought since you go my way anyway, you wouldn't mind."

They started to walk together.

"They've been bothering you out of school, too?"

"Yes."

"You're on The Rustlers turf, aren't you?"

"Yes."

"They're scum. But we'll manage 'em."

"I'm scared to get you in trouble with them."

"Don't worry about me. I used to belong to the rottenest gang in town. The Eleventh Street Scourges. All the punks in school know it, too, and they're never sure how

51

dangerous I might be. They suspect I can be vicious. They're right." He laughed sourly. "They respect that about me. They know I'd kill them without a qualm if it came to that. I must be scaring you more than they do."

"Oh, no. With you I feel absolutely safe."

"But to speak of pleasant things, Mimi, you're a charming girl. Just the kind of kid sister I'd have liked. Somebody was telling me you're a musician. Violin?"

"Piano."

"What field? Classics?"

"Yes. Bach . . . Beethoven . . . Schumann . . ."

"And Chopin's your favorite?"

They were standing on a curb waiting for a traffic light and he said it looking amusedly across her shoulder. Her mouth gaped.

"How did you know?"

"Simple . . . let's cross the street . . . if I'd had a charming little sister who played the piano, her favorite would have been Chopin. Because we'd never have disagreed about music . . . or, anything."

"Then he's your favorite, too?"

"Now, wasn't *that* brilliant of you," he said cuttingly. "Ah, now, I'm sorry. Don't be mad at me. I couldn't resist it. Don't feel stupid. You're not. Smile it up."

"O.K.," she laughed. "Well, this is my street." She glanced anxiously down it, then back at Mr. Wilks. "It looks all clear. I'll be all right."

"I'd better walk you on to your place."

"Well, if you wouldn't mind too much."

At the stoop she bit her lip and said in an urgent, hoarse voice, "This is the very last favor, but would you go up with me?"

He looked at her almost suspiciously for a moment. Then he pocketed his sunglasses and nodded tersely.

"Let's go."

Everything was all right . . . at least with him there it was. Nonetheless she was breathless when they got to her door.

"Is anyone home, Mimi?" He looked closely at her.

She shook her head.

"Are you all right?"

"Just nervous. Emotional. I'll be fine, though. Please don't think I'm crazy. Or just pretending I was scared to get you to walk with me. A girl around here has got a right to be jumpy. Do you understand?"

"Do I understand!" He laughed harshly. "You get on inside, now. I'll wait till you do." While she was unlocking the door he patted her shoulder. "Be careful of yourself, Mimi. I wouldn't want anything to happen to you."

She turned impulsively and hugged him, pressing her cheek to his chest. Then she went in and put on the chain lock.

"See you tomorrow," he called, and went down. She went to the window, opened it and leaned over the sill to watch him come out. She waved when he looked up. She watched him clear out of sight with a great sense of peace in her breast.

She went to the piano and practiced a full hour. To her, except for the out of tune strings, it sounded marvelous. She finished off with a high sense of accomplishment and well-being. Her timing was off, her touch erratic, and all in all she played with less ability than she'd displayed three years before. But Mimi didn't know it.

❖ SIX ❖

EVERY DAY FOR A WEEK Mr. Wilks escorted Mimi home safely. One afternoon several Rustlers were outside the candy store. Seeing them Mr. Wilks's stride got short and choppy. His whole body bristled. He stared at one, then another and then another of them, his expression coldly aggressive. Mimi thought they would never get past. When they did, one of the Rustlers snickered. Immediately Mr. Wilks whipped around.

"Did somebody say something to me?" he asked challengingly.

They all gazed at him blankly, then looked at each other, grinning. He went on.

Inside her building she whispered in awe: "Honestly, you're fearless!"

"Nobody's fearless," he snapped, not at her, but because he was very tense. She glanced at his face, but he gave her a warning frown not to stare, not to see that he was disturbed. He was calm when they reached her door.

"It's the old divide and conquer trick. Fix on one of them. Let him think he'll be the special target. Make as many as possible think he'd be the first to get hurt if something started. It makes them think. Thought, naturally, is poison to minds like theirs."

Another day, two of them entered the building right behind her and Mr. Wilks and climbed up toward the second floor as they did.

Mr. Wilks turned around and brought something round out of his jacket pocket.

"Hello, boys," he said, very softly. He let the round something roll off his palm. It was a bicycle chain. He dangled it like a snake, and grinned down at Dutch and

54

Rocky. They stopped and just stood there. "I can't reach you from here. Come one more step, Dutch."

Dutch's face became bleak, his mouth mashing together, his eyes narrowing. He grasped the handrail. Defiantly he stepped up one step and waited.

"This far enough, *Mister* Wilks?"

"I think so."

Dutch came up one more step. He started to grin.

"Just right." Mr. Wilks said, his smile getting a little shaky. "Far enough."

"Rocky, whattaya think about a grown man coming on our turf and taking a little kid up and tossing her every afternoon while her old lady's gone?" Dutch spoke to Rocky behind him without turning his head. "I think we ought to beat the crap out of him. Unless, Mr. Wilks, you would rather reform, and walk quietly all in one piece out of here. It's that or the other, because you know you haven't got the showdown guts to do anything with that bicycle chain except carry it back to your bicycle and pedal away. We'll politely back off and leave you pass if you make up your mind before I count three." He began a rhythmic, jeering: "And a-one . . . and a-two and a . . . thu-ree—"

Mr. Wilks shouted: "Four . . . five . . . six," while his arm was rising and falling in slashing fury and he started down the steps. The two Rustlers ran, shielding themselves. He followed, lashing backhand, forehand, backhand.

"Get on upstairs," he said to Mimi when he returned. He was breathing rapidly and his face was flushed and splendidly handsome.

"This time," she said at the door, "you *must* come in. For coffee."

"No, I mustn't. If ever I went in there for one minute alone in an apartment with a young girl student I'd be dead. I'd lose my job. If those rats could fix it, I'd go to jail."

"Aren't you afraid to go back out, now?"

"Yes. No. Some. We'll see. Their style isn't open attack where there's a hundred witnesses. It'll be all right."

But she watched anxiously from the window. He went back out of his way to pass them at the candy store. He

55

stopped and talked to them all for several minutes. Nothing happened and finally he went on.

Friday afternoon, just two weeks after she'd returned to school, Mr. Wilks came jauntily out of the school building. He lit his cigarette, winked at Mimi and put on his sunglasses. His buoyancy as they went down to the walk was catching. She kept glancing at him expectantly.

"Good news," he said.

"Tell me," she said excitedly.

He strode on, inhaled and exhaled smoke and grinned at her.

"Armistice."

"Armistice?"

"I said that."

"Oh, you big tease!"

"With the Rustlers. You know the three we had trouble with in school Wednesday before last? I'd kicked them out of class. Two of them needed to get back in very bad. One's on probation. The other's getting heavy pressure at home to earn a diploma. You can figure out the rest."

"I can't. I can't. Tell me, I'm dying."

"I'm re-admitting them to my class. They understand that you're under my protection. If *any* Rustler bothers you I'll consider it a violation of the truce."

"Oh, Mr. Wilks! Oh, Mr. *Wilks!*"

He paused, took out his billfold, handed her a small piece of paper. "This is a pass for a piano recital in Town Hall tomorrow afternoon. Can you use it?"

"Can I? Oh, this is wonderful! Thank you very much, Mr. Wilks. It just means so *much* to me. I'll just love it."

"In the ordinary course of affairs," he said in a playfully elegant way, "I get bundles of these things. I'll put you on my give-away list. It's little enough to do for one's protégé. Next time I'll make it a pass for two if you've got someone you'd like to go with . . . perhaps your mother."

"Ordinarily she just goes to *my* recitals."

"That's right, you're a recitalist yourself."

She laughed. "Just Mr. Ceccini's pupils," she said diffidently. "In about a month. I wish my piece was a Chopin. It's Weber, but maybe I can change it if you'd come."

"Please don't count on that," he said.

"Oh," she laughed, "if you could have seen your look

56

of horror. Well, I won't count on it; I wouldn't do a thing like that to my protector. I want you to know how much I appreciate everything. When my mother sees this pass to a place like Town Hall, she'll be overjoyed with pleasure."

"That's a good thing to be overjoyed with."

"Well, you see when all my troubles are gone and everything opens up I get effusive and use extra words to say how I *feel*. I expect it's a trait that will disappear as I mature, don't you?"

"No."

"You *don't?*"

"It's feminine."

"I like to think of myself as very, very feminine; basically passive and yielding and respectful of masculinity. You're so masculine, Mr. Wilks."

"Thanks."

"Oh," she giggled, "you're just trying to talk like a telegram to be in contrast with me. You're fun, you know that? Oh, I just wish you could meet my mother. She's such fun, too, when she's happy. And nothing makes her happier than a man she can respect. She, too, is very feminine. I'm not bragging, but she's the prettiest thing. Very very blue eyes and a lovely figure, and nice long legs and she's witty and her background . . . before we got broke and had to temporarily take this kind of apartment . . . was really quality. And she's only th . . . twenty-nine years old. You're about thirty, huh?"

"I've seen her."

"Then you know. I've got a sudden brilliant flash. Are you free Sunday afternoon? Do you like really sumptuous food?"

"I've got another engagement."

"Oh."

"Sorry."

Dressing to go to the Town Hall recital, Mimi changed her mind about her hair so many times her mother got exasperated.

"I thought you said this god (j. g.) wouldn't even be there."

"But if he is I don't want him to be ashamed. Do you know that teachers don't make such bad money, mother?

57

And they have steady, secure jobs. He thinks you're very good-looking. And he thinks you're only twenty-nine instead of thirty-two. Could we have him to Sunday dinner? He can't tomorrow, but next week?"

"I don't like him."

"Why, you've never even *seen* him."

"So?"

"Oh, mother, darling, you *couldn't* be jealous."

Her mother blinked. "I believe I am at that. Well, what do you know!" She grinned suddenly. "Silly of me, but I'm not a bit more immature than you were when you were five or six."

"Oh, that's good." Mimi laughed delightedly. "No more immature than I was at five or six . . . how was I then?"

"Jealous. If we'd be too nice to your little friends or praise them, whew!"

"How'd I act?"

"Adorable. But don't get me going on that or you'll be late. Run along and have a wonderful time. Tomorrow *I'll* give you a treat. The zoo. Then a movie. Sound good?"

"I'll like it better than today," Mimi assured her. "Bye-bye."

Her primping was wasted. He wasn't there. But the recital was inspiring. The pianist's level of achievement was galaxies beyond her present ability. But in his fourth number, a Bach prelude she too played, he made mistakes, and it gave her a gorgeous feeling. As brilliant as he was he could make mistakes! She loved him for it and applauded so hard her palms itched all the way home.

It snowed next day and her mother was furious with the weather for spoiling their plans.

The awful scene came Thursday. Mr. Wilks was still walking her home. He didn't entirely trust the Rustlers. Also, Mimi was privately convinced, he had come to enjoy her company. The day was unpleasant, sloshy underfoot, and half-rain half-snow was falling from a dirty, foggy sky. They both walked squinting, and when they came up onto the stoop they didn't see anybody in the mail foyer.

But she saw them, and she was half drunk. She just stood there with her legs apart, her coat pushed back, her hands on her hips and looked at one of them, then the

58

other, with an expression that grew nastier by the instant.

"Mother! You're home."

"Don't mother you're home me!" She tossed her head and sneered. She glared up at Mr. Wilks. "What're you pulling with my kid, you big son of a bitch?"

"Mother!" Mimi cried in shock. She caught her arm, looked pleadingly at Mr. Wilks. "Goodbye," she said hastily.

He nodded and turned to leave. Mimi's mother flung Mimi's arm off with a violent gesture and grabbed out with both hands and caught Mr. Wilks's overcoat sleeve and tugged him around. She stood glaring up at him.

"You never answered me."

"Nothing, Mrs. Danforth. I'm not pulling a thing. I give you my solemn word on that. As Mimi has probably told you, the hoodlums on this street frighten her. I've been seeing to it that they don't annoy her."

Mimi's mother kept staring at him fixedly. Suddenly she smiled that irresistible smile. Only it was like a grotesque carricature. She put out her hand and said simperingly: "My Name's Diane, Tom."

"Hello, Diane. I've been wanting to meet you. Mimi's told me so many good things about you." His smile was fixed and sick and he didn't look at Mimi.

"You talk like a gentleman. And you look . . ." She stepped back to get a better view and stumbled. She flailed, off balance. Mimi took her arm. Her mother giggled. "Mommy's had a couple too many. That's when to celebrate, right, Mr. Wilks? When you NEED to? Not when something's good."

"What happened, Mother?" Mimi said anxiously. She touched her mother's cheek. "Shouldn't we get on upstairs?"

"Isn't she a doll? Isn't she a sweet little doll? I mean, really, Mr. Wilks? I ask you, isn't she though? I mean, no, really, she is. What you wouldn't know from only knowing her in school is her lovely sympathy. Well, baby, I'm sorry, they canned me. It hadda come. Come on up, Tom. We'll get a jug and . . ."

"I really have another engagement. I was telling Mimi . . ."

"Like hell."

"He was. He's got an appointment. Honest, Mother."

59

"Sly. Sly. Got your stories together real sly. What *is* this?" She thrust her face directly at Mimi's. Mimi pulled back, fanning her face. "So I'm drunk. That's not the question. You still got it?"

"What?"

"I ask you a question. You got it?" She whirled on Mr. Wilks. "I ask YOU. You get it yet? Or are you building it slow?"

"Neither one."

" 'Cause, hell's bells and little fishes, there ain't time . . . . you know the September Song?"

"Mother, please."

". . . *no time for the waiting game*. You're right, honey, I sing like a crow." Suddenly coquettish, she moved clear up against Mr. Wilks and grinned up at him. "You're all right, you know that? You're a good-looking Joe. You like me?"

"You're a very attractive woman, Mrs. Danforth."

"Diane, honey. Diane. A goddess was named that. You know what my husband used to say about my figure? I'll whisper. Lean down. . . ."

Mimi thought she would faint. Her face became scarlet as her mother actually pushed herself against Mr. Wilks and looked up at him like a slut. She rushed into the inside hall and stood with her back turned, wishing she could sink through the floor.

Somehow Mr. Wilks must have got away. Her mother came in and slid an arm around her. "I got rid of the son of a bitch, baby. Don't worry. Mommy will chase all of 'em off that's trying to get her baby's innocence. What're you bawling about?"

"I'm not. . . ."

"You are, too. Your eyes are runny. I'll bawl, too," she said and began to cry aloud. Mimi finally got her upstairs and quieted down and then helped her into bed.

While her mother slept, Mimi studied in the front room. She sat with her legs tucked up into the armchair, books and notebooks on the piano bench in front of her. She began to need a sweater, but hunched her shoulders instead; she squinted more and more as it got darker and darker. Street lights from below the windows threw a little light on the ceiling.

60

She finished all her homework without having to turn on a light. Then she sat peering out at the dismal snow that completely blanketed the familiar mid-Manhattan tower lights. Some of the snow was floating down fatly and some of it rushed thinly upward on a draft. Her mother coughed. Mimi extricated herself from books and bench and hurried to her bedroom, her eyes sparkling with the thought that she was feeling better and getting up. But she lay soddenly, her sleep heavy.

It got to be seven and then seven-thirty. Mimi put on an extra sweater and stood in the dark in the kitchen and lit a gas burner and looked at the star-like pattern and then at the fascinating individual flames, little cones of purple-blue-orange-white; warmed her hands and then set the coffee pot on. She didn't get milk or sugar, just drank it black and bitter for its warmth.

She should turn on a light; it was spooky in the gaslight. She should *do* something, not just stand around life-stopped while the sands of time ran out. She took her left thumb, then forefinger, middle, third and little fingers in her right hand and cracked all the knuckles. She went through her right hand fingers. Well, she thought, that was doing something.

She went to the kitchen sink and washed her hands. She came back and heat-dried them. She bunched her finger-tips and kissed them in Mr. Ceccini's Italian way, then flung her hand out in a wide gesture, the whole thing meaning "Bravo!" "Bellissima!" "What a musician! You have it HERE . . ." she tapped her breast. Or here, she thought, mentally tapping her temple, a vacuum.

Nature adored, or was it abhorred, a vacuum. And where he could go if he didn't like her mother was to hell. She saw his disdainful mouth daring to sneer. Mimi's eyes glittered. Unconsciously her thin neck angled forward, her soft small chin jutted pugnaciously. Her sudden rage against him was all consuming; it swallowed up every other dislike and aggravation and pain and uncertainty and loneliness and fear. She went to her mother's bedroom and stood vowing passionate loyalty. She kissed her half-concealed face and patted her covers. Her mother stirred and turned, whimpering a little in her sleep. Mimi tiptoed out.

61

It was the longest, emptiest evening.

About ten she began to notice all the building's noises, all the raucous TV sounds, the people shouting, moving around, and she thought she couldn't bear it, being in this trap, this ugly, hateful, cramped, dirty prison. She thought of the endless, empty beautiful space, space, SPACE out west in the wide open spaces and let her thoughts drift along on a little story about herself she'd been imagining ever since that trip out west.

As always she was grown up but young, and she was in the kitchen of a big old frontier house in the cow country and she was singing and the sun shone golden on her hair which hung in two long, sweet, old-fashioned braids with blue ribbons and she was baking homemade bread for the cowhand's supper. From the distance a handsome stranger in a white hat and on a huge, shining black horse came riding across the plain at a walk. No, a lope. No, she changed it. At a wild, breakneck speed with the horse low and stretched out and foam-flecked. The stranger was swivelled around in the saddle firing two six guns at a mob of pursuing riders . . . Rustlers! . . . . Oh, damnit; she let her breath out in an exasperated hiss of anger . . . . there went *that* nice-feeling fairy tale she'd liked so well!

She had to eat. She turned the light on, sat down with a half loaf of bread, crackers, a jar of peanut butter, some milk, cold leftover pan of baked beans and ate and ate. If only her mother would wake up and they could just talk together and look in each other's eyes and see how they loved each other and know everything would be all right.

She hopped up as she heard her mother go to the bathroom.

"Hello," Mimi said from outside the door.

"What time is it, Mimi?"

"About eleven. Do you feel all right?"

"Just an aching head. Couple of aspirins'll fix it. Where are they?"

"The aspirins? Omigosh, I've been taking them. I'm sorry. They're all gone."

Her mother came charging out. Mimi backed away so fast she hit the wall. Her mother stopped.

"What ails you? You'd think I beat you." She reached out and patted her and suddenly Mimi collapsed, sobbing helplessly.

She slept with her mother that night. When Mimi got up her mother had done the housework and made breakfast and she looked so fresh and pretty, it was amazing.

"It did me good," her mother said lightly. "Sometimes it'll do that, ease off all your tensions. I'm chargey, today. What do you bet I have a job before noon?"

"I *know* you will, Mother."

✧ SEVEN ✧

MIMI TRIED to ignore Mr. Wilks in class next day. He stopped her afterward.

"Friends no more?"

"May I go? I'm ashamed and humiliated enough."

"Wait after school. That's an order. You may go now."

Of course she wanted to obey him, and she waited.

"The trouble with nice girls," he said edgily as they started to walk home, "is that under the sweet surface they're sour with selfrighteousness. Intolerant!"

She looked at him, puzzled. "You don't like me, is that what you're trying to say?"

"That may be," he said tightly. "I can tell you this. I was ashamed of *you* when you spoke of being ashamed and humiliated. Because, I suppose, of your mother's lapse."

Mimi veered over to an empty stretch of wall and leaned back against it. She watched solemnly as he came over, dragging at his cigarette.

"I was scared you'd have contempt for my mother. If you had had I was going to hate you. Now Mr. Wilks, don't be scared by what I'm going to say. It won't obligate you in the slightest. It won't be a burden on you. But when you said you were ashamed because you thought I was ashamed of my mother, which I'm not, I suddenly fell in love with you."

He whistled. *"Hate. Love!* Excuse me, what lies under the sweet surface isn't intolerance. Rather, melodrama."

She began to walk again. "I told you it wouldn't burden you," she said calmly. "I mean it. I don't expect any fulfillment of any kind. I want you to know of my love because just knowing someone loves you is like food. It makes you stronger to know you've earned something like

64

that, even from a person you don't respect. Even from an animal. Isn't that true?"

"Come in here," He steered her into a little grocery, opened a cooler, took out two Cokes, uncapped them and paid the clerk. He came back to Mimi.

"Let's drink," he said, almost grimly, "to dropping the whole subject."

On the street again Mimi walked with downcast eyes. She started to grin.

"That's better," he laughed.

"I was thinking," she explained, "how funny it would be to take your wife into a bar for a drink and she wouldn't be old enough."

During the next week they became better friends than ever. It was as if now that he knew the worst and wouldn't be plagued by it he could relax. And anyway, it was true, she knew secretly, that whether he'd admit it or not, the fact of her love enriched him.

Day by day through the week her mother's spirits went downhill as she didn't get a job. They didn't talk about it. They were very warm and close to each other. Her mother was late getting home Friday night. Mimi couldn't believe it was serious, but she worried as the evening went on and her mother didn't show up.

She put on her coat and galoshes and went down and stood on the stoop for awhile, then in the mail foyer, then on the stoop again. Nobody much was on the street. The Rustlers had a basement clubroom a few houses down on the other side of the street, and she could hear them in there. She walked down to the Avenue. It was cold and there was some snow at the edges of the walk. She went back to their building, becoming more numb with physical and emotional cold as the minutes crawled sickly along.

If her mother had a drink or so she might be this late. Or later. There wasn't any more to it than that. The candy store closed. The grocery at the other end of the block closed. Mimi went rapidly upstairs, thinking that when she'd been at one Avenue her mother might have come from the other direction, or someone had driven her home. The apartment was empty.

There hadn't been an accident. She was lithe and shot through traffic like mercury and couldn't get hit, and she'd

65

see a skid coming and get out of the way. So she hadn't had an accident. Mimi laughed at the very idea, which was impossible. She remembered her mother once going in for a drink at a bar near the movie. She set out for the few block walk, and went into the place. Everybody stared at her and she got right out without having the common sense to ask if they'd seen her mother. She went in four other places on the walk back home. She hurried, sure her mother would have arrived meantime. She hadn't.

Tom Wilks would know what to do! Mimi headed for his apartment, three blocks from her building. His building was much nicer, and you couldn't get in without a key. She pressed his bell. Presently there was a buzz, she pushed the door open. When she started up, he stood on the landing above in a pair of light slacks and a lavender satin lounging jacket.

"It's me."

"What is it, Mimi?" he inquired coolly.

"Mother didn't come home," she said, reaching him. "I'm awfully worried. It wouldn't be hysterical to call somebody official, would it?"

"My God, no. It's almost midnight!"

He beckoned impatiently and she followed him into his apartment, very attractively furnished, she noted. He sat at the phone table.

Mimi stood by nervously as he dialed. "I didn't know who to call. I mean there's so many hospitals . . . would notifying the police . . ."

He held up a silencing hand, spoke into the phone, very calmly, distinctly. He gave her address, her mother's name and said sharply to Mimi:

"What was she wearing?"

When Mimi told him he passed it on, then gave an almost perfect height-weight-build-age-hair-eyes description of her mother. At last he hung up and indicated a sofa.

"Sit down. They'll check and phone back in case she's hurt and in a hospital. She was carrying identification, I suppose."

Mimi sat stiffly in her coat, hands on her knees, and nodded.

"Which means you'd have been notified if anything bad had happened," he said, then observed, "You need gloves."

66

"I forgot them." She burrowed her reddened hands out of sight up her sleeves. He went into another room and came back with a pair of his own knit wool gloves.

"Unbutton your coat till you go out again, then wear these gloves. You can't be walking alone this time of night." A buzzer rang. "I had some guests coming." He went to the door, pressed a button, then he went out in the hall. He came back with two young men just as the phone rang. He came rushing to it. He stood listening, nodding, looking at Mimi, at the two men, who stood in the doorway looking at them both expressionlessly.

He hung up the phone, explained to the men: "This is a girl in one of my classes who lives near. Her mother's missing . . . I think I'll have to take her to the precinct station and make a Missing Persons report."

"That's all right," one of them said angrily; the other looked sullen. "Chuck and I'll push off."

"No. No. Hang around. I'll be back in no time," Mr. Wilks said urgently. He hurried over, almost forcibly closed the door, holding one of their arms. "Don't go. I'll call a cab and be right there and back in no time. Mimi, you call the cab. Chuck, Larry, there's wine, liquor, mixes . . . . make yourselves anything you want. O.K.? You'll stay?"

One of them shrugged, both went over and dropped slouchily onto the sofa, while Mimi called the cab. Mr. Wilks rushed into another room, came out putting on his coat, and looking at the men anxiously.

"It couldn't be helped. You understand?"

They didn't answer.

The trip to the station, talking to the detective who filled out a form, and Mr. Wilk's extreme nervous impatience were nightmarish. He dropped her off at her place in the cab and rushed away. All in all she felt a dreadful nuisance. She got a little sleep. Early next morning two detectives came and talked to her. She finally started to cry and admitted her mother could be on some kind of party. There was no word all day Saturday or all night.

Sunday morning Mr. Wilks came over. His nervousness was gone and he was very patient and cheering. He talked and talked. She couldn't say anything, she was so depressed she just couldn't even act polite. He went away but an hour later he was back with some pills. Mimi took

67

them and slept and woke feeling worse. It was night again.

He sat peering at her tenderly.

"Nothing?" she asked him.

"Sorry."

"What time is it?"

"Just after ten. If she was on a weekend party it will be breaking up now. People have to get to work Monday."

"That's so."

At midnight he took her out to eat. They left a note that they'd be right back. In the cafeteria he said:

"I'll phone a woman friend of mine and have her stay all night with you."

"Please don't. No. I don't want that. And you go home, too. It's my problem. It'll be over soon. But, Mr. Wilks. . . ." Her face started to crumple. Her eyes burned. "She never did this. She never did anything like this. What if she never comes back?"

"She will."

"If she'd only phone . . . . I mean," her mouth quivered. "Send a telegram. To let me *know*. I just don't know what to think or—or *do*."

He got her home again and stayed there with the door open till one o'clock . . . two o'clock . . . . Mimi lay in a miserable huddle unable to sleep. Mr. Wilks smoked cigarette after cigarette. He came and sat on the sofa, and petted her.

"She'll be here."

"You're my best friend." She looked at him miserably, her eyes glistening with tears. "You're the only friend I've got." She started to cry again.

"Try not to cry, Mimi. You're exhausting yourself . . ."

"She doesn't want me. She wishes she didn't have me. She can't get a husband with a brat into the bargain. She can't bring friends here on account of me. She wishes she never had had me."

"Don't think like that. It'll get you in such a state you'll be sick."

"Of course she loves me. She can't help *that*. But what am I *good* for? Something to get in her way. Something she has to support and who interferes with her life and fun. I'll never be worth the trouble anyway. When my

68

Daddy was alive . . ." She couldn't go on. She wept hysterically.

Finally she realized she was upsetting Mr. Wilks to the point where he'd start wishing she didn't exist, too. She sat up, her eyes raw, her nose red.

"Oh, well," she said.

People had started to get up for work in the building. It was nearly five o'clock.

"There she is! I hear her." Mimi leaped to her feet.

She rushed out and ran wildly down the stairs.

Her mother's face was dirty, lipstick-smeary. Her clothes were a mess. She didn't have on any stockings, one leg was cut. Mimi stood off a pace from her, frowning. Her mother scowled.

"You get your eyes full?" she demanded coarsely.

Mimi broke and ran into her arms, hugging her. Her mother didn't push her away but remained stiff and didn't embrace her. They went upstairs together, but heartachingly apart. Mr. Wilks had got out, she saw him on the floor above. He put a finger to his lips. Mimi went in with her mother, who went right to the bathroom, then to bed. Mimi followed.

"Don't start giving me hell!" her mother snapped. "I'm beat."

"Where," Mimi began.

"Where and who with is *my* business. So I'm a slut, so what?" She slammed her door.

Next evening Mimi bathed, dressed in all her nicest things and without a qualm lied to her mother about where she was going. Carrying a notebook on which she'd been working in school all day she went to Mr. Wilks's apartment. Fortunately he wasn't expecting anyone and was glad to see her.

He took her coat and exclaimed over her Sunday best clothes. The small gray bonnet type hat matched her two-piece suit. The suit jacket was a bolero type that didn't button and exposed her pink satin blouse, which was old and getting tight on her but smart and expensive. While she waited he went in and made some tea and brought it on a tray with some English muffins he'd toasted and there were jellies.

They sat across from each other enjoying the food and

saying nothing. She knew that speech between them was not necessary; she believed that if they'd been struck dumb they could go through life in total silence, but communicating perfectly. Her eyes paused from time to time on some one particular feature of his . . . the angle formed by his forehead and temple, the flare of his nostrils, and loved him so greatly that if the chance should come she would become his indentured servant or his slave. She would work for him without pay, without reward, without a kiss or a caress or a touch; just for the glory of being near him and belonging to him.

When they finished he lit a cigarette. "How's the weather at home?"

"Better. Of course she's sorry."

"They always are."

"Not that she isn't sincere."

"True."

"I've come here for a serious purpose, Mr. Wilks."

"Let me get these things cleared away. Then we'll get to it."

"I'll help."

"Nothing to it. Just wait here."

He came back, got comfortable on the sofa, patted the place beside him. "Or would you rather have that chair and face me. Incidentally, those little white bows you have in your hair at the temple are quite attractive. And a bit of lipstick tonight, too, eh?"

"Yes," she said solemnly. "I'd prefer to remain on my feet. And may I remove my jacket?"

"Oh, so formal? You have my permission."

She had unbound her breasts, and they thrust, conical and separately defined, against the lustrous pink satin. She stood in profile, showing him, and gazed across her shoulder.

"Do you notice?"

He sat forward, took her hand and said gravely. "Why, Mimi? Why do you imagine you need falsies? It's because of what you've been through. You're badly upset, dear."

She cupped her hand under one breast. "This is *me!*"

He smiled affectionately. "Remember, I'm your best friend. You don't *need* to lie to a best friend. Those things don't sprout overnight like that. Yours will come in good time. Meantime, just be you."

She turned to face him. "I was binding myself so I wouldn't attract boys' attention. But I don't want to be hidden from *you*. Put your hand up here and feel for yourself if this isn't flesh—warm flesh, tender with love."

"Mimi!"

"I'll show you, then."

"No, you won't, Mimi. Because I'm asking you not to. If this is the state you're in, I'll have to take you home. Though I don't want to, because I enjoy your company and like you very much. You worry me, Mimi."

"Wait," she said urgently and walked over to her overcoat and got her notebook from the pocket. She came back to the middle of the room. She opened the notebook, gazed at him, then began to read:

"A list of my qualifications. One. Clean. Two. Neat. Three. Punctual. Four. Honest. . . These items aren't arranged in groups the way I would like them, so that mental and emotional and physical qualities are all mixed up. Anyway Five. Capable of enduring hardship. Six. Able to do without small immediate pleasures. Seven. Hopefulness. Eight. Cheerfulness. Nine. Seriousness. Ten. Capacity to learn, improve, change for the better. . . ."

"Mimi, what *is* this? Honey, what are you *doing?*"

"Proving I'd be worthy of being your wife."

"Wife!" he cried. He got agitatedly to his feet, stared into her eyes. "You're serious."

"I'm beyond puberty and therefore capable of bearing children and I have," she flipped pages in the notebook, "item 75, maternalism."

He took the notebook, read it frowningly, glancing occasionally at her solemnly lovely little face.

"I'm not so silly," Mimi said, "as to think a list like that would mean anything. Mainly, I love you with all my heart. I would do everything in my power to be the best wife in the world."

"I believe you," he said seriously. "But, Mimi. . . ."

She broke in. "In Southern states I'm old enough to marry."

He shook his head slowly, his eyes compassionate.

"Mr. Wilks, from what you've done for me, and by the sweetness in the way you look at me, I know that you love me. In history, girls younger than I am were passionately loved, and became wives."

71

"I'm touched. Impressed. I don't doubt the genuineness of your feelings, understand. But the whole situation. . . ."

Mimi stepped close to him. She slid her hands up his chest and over his shoulders to curve around his neck. He drew back, shaking his head, but her fingers laced together. He took her elbows and tried to break her grip without hurting her. She clung to him, and her lifted face glowed. The shining gaze of her widened eyes fixed on him with compelling intensity.

"Kiss me, darling," she whispered. "You're so good, so fine, so clean, so loving . . . love me . . . love me . . ."

She sighed and closed her eyes so that her lashes lay like rich lace above the satiny roundings of her soft cheeks and her fresh, warm lips parted slightly, looking faintly swollen.

She felt his hands relax around her elbows, glide to her shoulders and then follow the narrowing bowing contours of her upper back down to her waist, embracing and stroking. His touch sent actual shivers of pleasure over her sensitive skin.

She stepped an inch forward, her vibrant young body a yielding arch merging with the solid bulk of his strong male body. His possessing, protecting strong hands held her more tightly, and she felt his face lowering to hers. She began to tremble with anticipation. His mouth touched hers with an exquisite, tiny friction like velvet on velvet and a shimmery, quickening sensation raced through her.

She pushed her face upward, opening her lips under his. Her arms dropped from his neck to his back and she clutched him fiercely, mashing her breasts on the hardness of his chest. Her heart pounded giddily and a throbbing began in her lips and her nipples tingled as if stabbed painlessly by a hundred needles.

His hands were moving up and down her back, touching her hips. She crowded herself closer. She freed her lips, gasping, then her mouth blindly sought his again and he was deep kissing her and her tongue darted, responding. She could feel the heat of his body against her. Almost feverishly she turned herself, pulling him around. She held to him and sat on the sofa. He broke free and stood up panting, shaking his head, wiping his mouth.

"Sit down. Sit by me . . . Please, please," she begged

in a husky, passionate voice. She sat lengthwise on the sofa, one leg extended, the other drawn up, exposing her knee. He sat on the edge beside her. She began to unbutton her blouse.

"No, Mimi," he said hoarsely, and seized both her hands. She freed one hand, caressed his cheek, his neck, his forehead.

"I love you. . . . I love you. . . . Love me, Tom. You must." She had two blouse buttons open. With both hands she drew his hands to her breast. "Put your hand on my bare breast. Touch me . . . Please."

She looked feverish. Her eyes were brilliant. She kept wetting her throbbing lips. Her cheeks were bright pink; a heavy pulse fluttered at the base of her throat. She struggled with his hand while he pulled back and yielded in spasms. When at last she felt the slight roughness of his hand on the sensitive skin of her breast, stroking, caressing, she shivered with ecstasy.

"Look at my breasts. They're beautiful, they're for you!"

She yanked her skirt up to the edge of her panties showing him the soft young loveliness of her naked thighs.

"Touch me there, too. Touch me everywhere. I'm all yours, dearest, darling!"

Abruptly he stood up and walked to the other side of the room. Mimi ran after him crying out and flinging her arms around him, her face distraught. She was trembling all over.

He pulled her arms loose and thrust her away. He looked at her warningly.

"Stop this."

She must have the beauty of his love to wipe out the ugliness of that rape.

"You don't understand," she cried passionately. "It's not marriage I want. Not that. Just love! I *must* have your love. I *must*." She fell to her knees and clasped her hands and implored him. "Make me clean with your love. I need you. The goodness of your love, your flesh in my flesh. Let me feel your love, let me give you love. . . ."

He almost ran out of the room. She got up and started after him. He came back with a glass of water and sloshed it in her face.

She went to a chair and dropped like a stone. She just

sat, staring up at him, her face, dripping water, becoming pale.

"You won't?"

He turned, went over and got her coat.

"Come on."

"Do you think I'm insane?" she said in a hushed voice.

"No. But I am not going to go to bed with you."

And she knew why. *He loved her too much.*

The next time she went for her music lesson Mr. Ceccini was in a fret. He listened and paced, and shook his head, till she was nervous. She stopped playing, dropped her hands to her lap.

"You're mad because I wasn't able to get the money."

"No. No. No." He made wiping motions in the air with both hands. "It's not that. Only what happened that you didn't bring what you owe to me?"

She explained, as she'd had to more than once in the past. "But didn't I always catch up?"

"True. Now to see if you can get past mechanics and grasp the music. Bach did not put down notes to test the FINGERS. Musical idea and feeling is to be expressed."

"Well, I know that," she said in a tone of injury.

"I know you ought to know that. Always you know that. Only the last two or three lessons, I didn't say it, but I can't believe my ears. I thought, so, only a young girl. Her boy flirted with another girl. Only a triffle. Then today, more worse."

Suddenly she giggled.

It angered him. "What is funny?"

"Triffle. You always pronounce it wrong. It's *tri*-fle."

"Oh! That's the thing your mind deals with? Amusements how a man from another country fails sometimes to speak correctly? We have no connection!"

"I'm sorry." She broke into giggles again. "I'll play it again. . . ."

"What's the good?"

"I didn't mean to laugh. It wasn't your saying 'triffle,' but what you were saying about my *playing*. If I didn't laugh, I'd cry," she said in sudden desperation. "I know I never have played better. I just KNOW my music is IMPROVING!"

74

He stared at her. "You think I am against you; to tell you a lie because I don't like you?"

"No. But."

"I wouldn't lie to an enemy. Not concerning *music*."

"What should I *do?* I swear to you I've worked as much as I could . . . almost as much as usual. And I was sure I was making great strides, Mr. Ceccini. You told me I'm a musician. You know you did. So I am! I've got a *future* in music. You said!"

"Yes. So. Be calmer, bambina, more calmer. You should have a rest. A few weeks don't play. Force yourself to not play. Deprive yourself of it. Then it will be needed to you and dearer to you. The talent then returns. . . . Meantime . . ."

She gathered up her things and ran out and went directly to Tom Wilks. She would tell him everything. About the rape that had killed the music in her, killed her judgment, killed her dreams. Then he would love her, and by his act of love, with his body pure within her body she would be good.

He stood in his doorway, blocking it.

"What do you want, Mimi?"

"May I come in?"

"No."

"Not even come *in?*"

He didn't say another word. He just stood there saying something by the disdainfulness of his mouth. What he said without a word was clear. He disliked her. She turned away and went to the stairs. She heard his door shut. She went home.

✦ EIGHT ✦

THEIR FIRST WELFARE CHECK had come. It was bitterly cold and snowing. She and her mother sat with extra sweaters on, reading and looking up at each other now and again. Mimi had something on her mind. She kept not saying it. She cleared her throat. Her mother looked up. Mimi looked down at her book.

"Mimi, what is it . . . . what do you want to tell me?"

"I think I'm pregnant."

"You are not!" her mother said, her face twisted in shock and disbelief.

"I am too!"

"You are not!" She said it like an order. "You don't know a thing about it." Her hands started flurrying around her lap and pockets as if she itched. She hopped up, searched the chair, found her cigarettes saying: "Your period's a day late, I suppose, so," she lit a cigarette, shook out the match flame, "a day or two late and . . . bam . . . hysteria!"

"It's several days late." Mimi stood up. "And I missed last month, too."

Her mother quaked as if she'd been delivered a low blow, then walked away. She came back. She seemed ready to accept it. Then her nostrils tightened and she tossed her head.

"And what does *that* prove? Emotional upsets throw things off. My vanishing that weekend was dreadful for you. You're insecure. Tense. This sort of thing can emotionally paralyze. Why, do you know that for months . . . as if my vital functions had stopped . . . for several months after your daddy died, my menstrual period was erratic. Mimi!" She drew herself up authoritatively, pointed a finger. "March to your room. I'm going to inspect you. And I'll tell you this, if you've gone behind my

76

back and done anything and if you're not a virgin, Mimi Danforth. . . ."

"Of course I'm not," Mimi shrilled. "How could I think I was pregnant if I was a virgin?"

"March to your room. This time I mean it. I'm going to punish you. I tell you, Mimi, you need it. You've got it coming. I mean I'll blister you till it soaks through, so that in the future. . . . Oh, Jesus God! Mimi, sweetheart, what good would *that* do? I just WISH it would solve it! When did it happen, baby?"

She told her the exact date.

"Well, it wasn't your fault, I know that much. I'll get him. I promise you that. Have you told him? What did he say? How'd he react?"

"You think it's Tom Wilks, but it isn't."

"Then, who?"

"Oh, what's the difference?" Mimi cried, "I should have known, I should have *known* if I'd turn to you everything would get worse, not better."

Her mother jabbed out her cigarette. "I had that coming. Well, I know a doctor," she said calmly. "There's tests to make absolutely sure."

Within the week the tests had confirmed that she was pregnant.

Miss Appleton, the nurse who took the lab samples, set up a first appointment with the doctor himself. As Mimi's mother explained it the kindly doctor's full-time uptown office catered to rich patients; he maintained the downtown place as a form of service to the poorer people. His fees were so low as to be near-charity. Which was why he didn't invest in a regular office there but used rooms behind a beauty parlor.

Miss Appleton, who also ran the beauty shop, greeted them and led them back past operators, and customers in booths and under driers. At the end booth, Miss Appleton pushed back the curtain and said to Mimi:

"You step in here, Miss Anderson, while your aunt's talking with the doctor." Mimi's mother had used a false name in making the appointment.

Miss Appleton gave her a loose white nightgown-like garment.

"Just remove your clothes, dear, and slip this on. And take these."

"What are they?" Mimi said, frowning at the pills.

"Relaxants."

"But I don't want to be sleepy when Dr.—I don't even know his name . . . asks me about my case. . . ."

"Ah, but the doctor doesn't know *your* real name, does he? As for your medical history, the madame, I mean your *aunt,* is telling him all he needs to know. He'll examine you internally. These pills make everything painless."

"Oh well, an ordinary examination won't hurt."

"Listen, make it easy on yourself. The medical instruments, the probes and all, you understand, they make you flinch. Unless the internal organs are relaxed good, the doctor can't examine you fully. The pills are doctor's orders, sweet, so you just take them, and hustle out of those clothes."

"O.K." She took one pill, palmed the other.

She undressed and got into the nightgown. She still had on shoes and stockings and wondered muzzily about that, but the pill had started to take effect and she had a kind of blurry indifferent attitude. Then Miss Appleton was leading her into the doctor's office. She could feel her mother's brief hand-squeeze but didn't see her.

She didn't like Miss Appleton or the office. There was a narrow table and a low cone light. She didn't like the doctor who didn't even say hello, just stood with his faceless face back of a surgical mask and obscure in the shadow above the cone light. She sat on the edge of the table. Her feet were put into some kind of stirrups, then her legs were being spread, her knees strapped. Miss Appleton lay her back on the table.

On a side table she saw gauze and pans of water and bottles of medicine and a horrid array of knives and needles and a wedge-like torture-looking device, probably to spread her apart, and a terrifying icepick-like thing. The doctor's rubber-gloved hands had her buttocks, lifting, pulling, pushing her into position. Then he sat down on a stool between her legs and reached for something on the side table and a raw chill ran through her flesh.

Mimi started to yell and try to kick her strapped legs. She clutched the side of the table and pulled herself up in a sitting position and hit at the doctor's chest, and screamed and fought Miss Appleton who tried to pull her back down. She felt herself falling backward, hitting her head. She bounced up again. She flung her upper body forward, and locked her arms to her legs, and stayed that way, shielding her privacy, and kept yelling at the top of her voice.

"Let me go . . . . let me loose . . . . let me *GO* . . . let me out of here."

"Get her out of here! Unstrap her. Get her out! Shut up, kid. We're letting you go. Shut up, or I'll *slug* you!"

She shut up when she felt the straps released from her legs. She jumped off the table and rushed for the door. It was locked.

"Open this door," she hissed.

Miss Appleton hurried over.

"Calm down . . . I'm letting you out. . . . There, it's unlocked. . . ."

Mimi dashed into the booth, pulling off the white garment. Naked, she began to get into her clothes, her teeth chattering. She was aware of her mother, agitated and frightened. Mimi looked at her with glazed eyes. Then everybody was helping her into her clothes, hurrying her and her mother outside.

On the street her mother ordered: "Stay right here. I'll be right back."

Mimi didn't stay. She walked as fast as she could in the general direction of a subway station. She found one, got a train and went home. She was sitting in the hall outside their apartment door when her mother arrived, frantic!

"Where'd you go? You all right?"

She got Mimi to her feet, unlocked the door, hurried her inside.

"I said you all right?"

Mimi was silent.

"At least I got most of the money back. You crazy kid, what ails you?"

Her mother gripped her shoulders and shook her. "You still doped? Say something. They didn't hurt you, did they?"

"You knew!" Mimi accused. "You knew he was an abortionist."

"Yes. But he's safe. I knew that. I didn't want to scare you."

"You lied. You lied!"

She wrenched free and backed away and stood against the piano and cried, "Don't touch me!"

"Honey," her mother appeased. "You're yelling. Don't advertise to everybody that . . ."

"I'll yell if I PLEASE. . . ." She screeched the last word. She clutched the piano back of her and tried to mash herself into it, retreating from her mother. "If you touch me I'll run to that window and jump out. I will." She stood, her face red, breathing very shallowly.

"I won't touch you."

Mimi's expression became one of loathing. She stared fixedly and unblinkingly at her mother's face and hated her. Hated her! Her mother saw the look in her eyes.

"Mimi," she whispered, seeming to shrink back. "Don't look at me like that. Baby, *don't* . . . I didn't know . . . I . . . I thought you'd be relieved . . . happy. . . ."

Mimi continued to stare grimly. Her mother's features drained as with shock.

"Please, Mimi." Suddenly she turned and fled from the room.

She was gone a long time. When she came back Mimi was sitting on the piano bench, looking at her hands, feeling limp all over.

"Deny it all you please," her mother said. "But the reason you want the baby is obvious. You're in love with Tom Wilks."

"Yes." Mimi didn't look up. She said slowly, distinctly, articulating each word separately, "But . . . he . . . is . . . . not . . . the . . . father."

"So protect him."

Mimi stood up and drew a deep breath. "Sit down. Go sit down, Mother. I'm going to tell you something that'll knock you down. Go on. Sit down. Listen."

Awed, her mother obeyed.

"Do you remember the night your boyfriend Mac tried to rape me, Mother? I screamed like a madwoman. Just from fright, just a hysterical little girl," she said in a hoarse voice. She smiled bitterly. "Would you like to know what had happened that very afternoon?"

80

"Oh, no, darling. . . ."

"Oh, yes! I was raped."

For a moment her mother just sat, the blood draining from her face till it was chalk white; her blue eyes wide and staring glassily. She wet her lips.

"Raped," she said in a soft hoarse voice. Suddenly she came streaking up out of the chair. "Raped!" Her hands curved, clawlike, then clenched. Color came flooding back to her face; Mimi could see the violent throb of pulse at her throat. Then she was drawing breath and saying savagely, "Why didn't you *tell* me? Report it. Come on. We're going to the police! They'll find him! *I'll* find him. I'll rip his filthy guts out." Her eyes glistened with tears of rage. "We'll make him wish he was dead! Oh, my darling, my darling! Come on! Don't stand there! We're going to get the cops on this thing. . . ."

"Wait!" Mimi caught her arm. "Please, mother! Why do you think I didn't tell anybody? I'm scared. They threatened. . . ."

"THEY!" her mother shrieked. "More than ONE. . . ?"

"Yes. And they'd kill me. I *know* they weren't bluffing. They're mean. Vicious! They've been in trouble before and got out. They'd be back, and they're dangerous! We *can't* go to the police. They might cripple me, kill me. . . . They were horrible, Mother. I'm terrified of them. . . . I know what they *are*. They got in here. They took all my clothes off right in here. Then they took me in to my bed. Spud . . . . Rocky . . . . Dutch . . . . another one I don't know his name. . . ."

"Not FOUR . . . . oh, my God."

"No. *SIX* . . . . *Every one of them.* They tore me open! I was killed and killed and killed. . . . And they left their scum in me. Now it's alive. Its father is vile, brutal scum. But IT won't be. *It's* mine. All mine! I *will* have it. I *will* love it! I *will* make it everything in the world they are not. And if I die at childbirth, *it will live!* Mother, you'll see to it that it becomes everything I wanted it to. Promise me that, Mother, with your hand raised. Swear to God, Mother, that you'll do that for me if I die. . . ."

"Oh, my baby, Mimi . . . . Mimi, you *won't* die."

"Promise me, Mother. Promise and swear!"

"Yes."

"Do it!"

"Yes, darling . . . relax . . . whatever you say . . . See, I raise my right hand. . . ."

❖ NINE ❖

AT THE END of the semester Mimi dropped out of school. In mid-February, a pleasant, homely woman from Welfare paid a call. After a few amenities she came to the point:

"We've had information that you quit school, Mimi."

"Yes."

"You aren't yet sixteen. You know, Mrs. Danforth, she's required to attend school."

"Well, let's face it, Mrs. Cobb, since we're going to be needing extra money for the event. Mimi is pregnant."

"I see," Mrs. Cobb said, looking at Mimi.

"I don't show much yet but I will. I thought I'd better stay out one semester."

"I suppose it would be embarrassing."

"Not only that. The kind of people who go to that school might haul off and kick me in the stomach."

"Oh, dear! I hope you *are* exaggerating. However, we can arrange for home study."

"Really? To get credits?"

"Oh, yes, dear. I'm so glad you want to," Mrs. Cobb sighed and opened a briefcase. "And now to the forms for the allowance increases. There'll be doctors, medicines, the layette. . . ." She seemed to brighten at the prospect and kept glancing at Mimi as if she'd become her favorite. "If you could give me an idea of when the child's expected. . . . I guess you'd rather not speak of the father. I'll put unknown."

Mimi's mother gave a short, harsh laugh. The women looked at each other.

"Shall I tell her, Mimi?"

"There's nothing I'd like better than to have them ar-

83

rested. You know that. But they're very vicious, and they warned me if I told. But . . . well," she decided. "I wish you *would* tell her." She got nervously to her feet and crossed the room. "I'd just rather not listen. . . . I'll wait in my room."

That afternoon two detectives came and practically begged them to come downtown and sign a complaint.

"If you let them walk free, knowing what they are, Mrs. Danforth, you're lining yourself up . . . not, of course, with any such intention . . . on their side against decent people . . . against your own little girl and God knows how many others. You see that."

"I see it. I hate them. I want them punished. But they *are* vicious and they threatened her. I didn't even find out about it for about two months, that's how terrified she was . . . and still is. I can't do it without Mimi's say-so."

"I've changed my mind," Mimi said suddenly. "I'm ready to go and make a complete statement and swear to it and sign it."

By nightfall every one of the six had been arrested.

She and her mother kept talking about it, pep-talking each other. When it came to a trial and testifying they'd go through with it. They had promises that the hearings would be closed; there'd be no newspaper publicity about it to smear Mimi.

The six were released on bail the same night they were taken in, but they were on their best behavior and didn't bother her or her mother. A trial date was set for two-and-a-half weeks later in Judge Broissard's chambers. Meanwhile, Mimi talked to teams of detectives from the police, the juvenile bureau and from the judge's own staff. They came to the apartment sometimes, at others she went to headquarters.

She went over the whole story and over specific parts of it so many times that it took on the feel of something that had happened to somebody else. She thought she couldn't be upset by it till one morning in the cubbyhole office of Mr. Sanders, the frowning, intense little court-appointed lawyer.

"You say you don't think Dutch was undressed . . . . nor Rocky . . . . nor Spud . . . . nor Doc. . . . How about the one you say giggles—Dopey?"

"None did. I told you. Why ask about each one separately?"

"Any scar, tattoo, specific oddity we could establish would help. I understand the emotional force of the occasion. But if you could focus on it and recall. . . ."

"This is too much!" Mimi's mother flared. "I don't want her forced to live any part of that horrible experience over."

"Please, Mrs. Danforth!"

"Mother, why don't you go over to that cafeteria and wait for me. Your listening in makes it harder."

Mr. Sanders offered her mother a cigarette, lit it for her. "Mimi's right, Mrs. Danforth. I know you want to help her. But your presence, added to her instinctive reluctance to endure that suffering again, even in words, makes it gruelling. We're concerned with justice, with stopping punks of that kind. Every detective you and the girl have talked to is convinced she's telling the whole truth. We have strong statements about her character from neighbors, from her music teacher, from teachers in her present and previous schools.

"We know she's not a . . . well, not that kind of kid. What the counsel on the other side is relying on is the fact that girls in trouble make unfounded accusations of rape. It's provable that intercourse occurred. The question is who with. *We* know. But proof . . . . especially since so much time has elapsed . . . . is hard to establish."

"I understand. I'll go have some coffee. And at the hearing I'll remember to hold tight, not get aggressive and prejudice the case against us. . . . I promise that."

"Now, Mimi," Mr. Sanders said, when they were alone.

"I remember that one did take off everything. I saw his whole body, his sexual arousal. . . ." She shut her eyes and grimaced. "It was clear to me. But I don't even know which one of them it was, I swear. There's no way I'd know if he was unusual."

"All right, kid, that's a dead-end. Now, about your opening that roof door. You *did* open it and because you opened it, they came in. They may claim you *let* them in for a party. I don't think they will. They're denying ANY contact with you. But could we go over one more time the minutes just preceding your opening that door?"

85

"Yes," she nodded and complied. When she had finished, she said: "Isn't it obvious they had it all planned out?"

"Yes. And we can establish that they went through a building three doors down from yours. Our only trouble is the witnesses can't swear to the exact date. However, five of the six have records and our word against theirs will be sufficient."

"You really think so, Mr. Sanders?" she stared earnestly across his desk. He was silent for a long while.

"Mimi, we're up against extra-legal factors. Undercover influences, politics, a lot of things. Frankly, the best we can do is hope."

She and her mother arrived with Mr. Sanders a half hour early the morning of the hearing. They, with several detectives, formed a group at one end of the old, gloomy corridor. The six Rustlers in company with eight or ten men and women, parents and lawyers, stayed at the other end. The boys wore suits and ties and showed meek, downcast faces.

A bailiff ushered Mimi's group into a dim high-ceilinged room lined with bookcases. The judge, a bland, middle-aged man, sat at a large desk, looking at a sheaf of papers in a file folder. When they'd taken seats along the ring of chairs facing him, he looked up, smiled and spoke to Mr. Sanders, leaned forward and said:

"I want you to know, Mrs. Danforth, that you have a girl to be proud of. There is no doubt in the court's mind whatsoever that hers is a case of innocence outraged. . . ." He went on for several minutes, speaking of all the good character information that had come in on Mimi and how concerned the court was to see that justice was done. Then Mr. Sanders seemed to catch some signal that Mimi missed, and he motioned them to go out.

Back in the corridor they watched the other group go in. Mr. Sanders was gloomy.

"It looks all right, doesn't it?" Mimi's mother asked him in an urgent whisper. He shook his head. "No. You heard the apology in His Honor's voice? He's with us, and he's sorry as hell. But the evidence isn't incontrovertible. Now keep hold of yourself, both of you. In a few minutes we'll be going back in there while those punks are there. Don't look at them. When the judge gives them a nasty tongue lashing, don't get your hopes up . . . or your temper!"

"You can trust us," Mimi said, gripping her mother's arm.

They were prepared. Nonetheless, when, after giving the Rustlers hell and warning them about their future conduct, the Judge placed them on probation, Mimi felt sick. The others filed out. The judge, after a few sympathetic words, left the room. Mimi, her mother and Mr. Sanders went out.

"I feel rotten," he said. "I'm sorry."

"You did all you could," Mimi said.

"Yes," her mother assured him. "Well, anyway, they'll be on their good behavior."

The whole gang of Rustlers, including the Rustlerettes, celebrated their freedom. They massed together and took a walk, forcing people to get out of the way. The whole pack stopped directly in front of their building.

"Yah yah yah . . . yah yah yah," they howled like animals, the female shrills chorusing with the snarly male shouts. "Yah . . . yah . . . yah . . ."

Mimi watched with her mother from behind closed windows.

"Look at them! I never knew human beings could be so ugly!"

Her mother just stood with transfixed eyes, her fists clenched. Finally two squad cars whined down the street and broke it up. For several days and nights teams of police patrolled the block with now and then a squad car cruising past. The police were withdrawn, but several different times Mimi and her mother passed a pair or a group of Rustlers without any sign of recognition or hostility.

"Their buddies in that bureau put them up to it," her mother commented. "Acting like they don't know you is supposed to prove they're innocent!"

"The good part of it is they're not bothering us."

"I'm glad you found something good about things; that's good sunbeaming, pet."

An official party for the Rustlers and two other gangs was to be given in a neighborhood hall. The afternoon of the party Mimi and her mother came home from the grocery and found chalked on a downstairs wall:

87

"Dollar whorehouse . . . follow Arrows."

Chalked lines studded with arrow points led upward. On their own door was chalked:

"Mimi $1 . . . Diane $1 . . . 2 for $1.79."

They got the marks wiped off. But all evening they were edgy.

About ten, her mother, cat-nervous, suddenly stiffened in her chair, her eyes rounding, her head tipping toward the hall. Mimi heard it too . . . a squeaking of a floorboard, but no footsteps. Both of them looked suddenly at the door. A strip of grocery-sack brown paper was sliding under. They just sat, looking at it, then at one another and not moving.

Finally her mother bolted, snatched up the paper. She read it, wadded it angrily, set her face grimly and stared at the door. Another strip came under. Her mother shrieked:

"You filthy scum!"

No answer. Mimi was on her feet, standing at her mother's shoulder. She put an arm around her.

"Don't open the door," Mimi whispered.

"Think I'm crazy?" She spoke to the blank door. "It's chain locked. Squat out there in your own manure all night long for all I care."

"Mimi. . . ." there was a loud whisper from the hall. "Mimi . . . it's your baby's daddy out here! Tom! Let's have another party."

Mimi hit the door with her fists. "Beat it. Get away, you dirty punks."

Her mother slipped from the room. Mimi ran after her, into her own bedroom. Her mother was staring at the airshaft window.

"I was scared they were using that front door gag to cover the sound of trying to get in back here. I guess they couldn't. It's all right."

They went back to the front room and stood looking at the door. After what seemed like an hour they decided nobody was out there. Still they didn't open the door. They went and had coffee in the kitchen. They came back, glancing at once at the bottom of the door. No more notes.

"They're gone," her mother said. "But I just wish I *knew.*"

88

"We could open it a peek, with the chain lock on."

"It'd be a relief to KNOW they're not out there."

Her mother turned the key, then the knob, unlatching the door. An abrupt weight thrust against the door. The chain slid and held, stretched. Together her mother and she hurled all their weight against the door, trying futilely to push it shut. They saw the short, thick open steel jaws of snippers close on the chain. The chain snapped.

Rustlers burst into the apartment, so many she couldn't count. Some swarmed around her, some around her mother. Mimi's struggles were brief and useless. She was gagged and held by two of them.

She saw her mother standing with adhesive over her mouth. Dutch and Spud flanked her, pinning her arms. Doc stood in front of her mother and smashed his fist into her jaw so hard her head hit her shoulder as if her neck broke. Mimi screamed into the gag.

"Wait," a voice near Mimi ordered. "The bitch shut her eyes. Open 'em, bitch, or we'll take a knife to her face and carve down to the bone. . . . Open your eyes!"

She opened her eyes and tried to plead but her words were a muffled strangling sound against the mouthful of cloth. Doc hit her mother in the stomach, making her double forward. She straightened and Dutch chopped the back of her head with his fist.

They flung her down on her face on the sofa and yanked her skirt up past her panties. One of them held her down with a knee in her back. Another whipped her with a strip of leather, hissing, vicious cracking blows. Blood began to show through her panties. They tossed her onto her back.

One straddled her and deliberately drove his fists into her breasts, left and right and left. Her mother's eyes above the adhesive looked like they were bursting out of the sockets. Mimi prayed she was unconscious. But her whole body jerked horribly with every blow. Two of them took her feet and stretched her legs wide apart, exposing her shamelessly. They bent her toes back brutally, twisted her ankles viciously. They dropped her legs, quit hitting her breasts. They left her and came to Mimi.

Dutch looked coarsely at her. He lit a cigarette. He dragged till the ember was bright. He blew off the dust of ash, brightening the ember further. Mimi held her breath, knowing he was going to burn her.

"Everybody light up," Dutch said. He moved the cigarette toward her face. Hands behind seized her head in a viselike grip. She squirmed, shut her eyes, opened them at once in terror. They felt raw. She whimpered and writhed. She could feel the heat on the tip of her nose. Dutch began to grin at her. He withdrew the cigarette, puffed. He looked proudly at his buddies.

"Now, Mimi. The second business with your old lady comes. We strip her naked. Then we put out our cigarettes. On her belly. Her breasts, her tail. Maybe her face. If you yell when we take off your gag, we do that."

The gag was removed. Mimi stood mute.

"Want us to do that to her?"

She shook her head, her tear-streaked face wretched.

"Who's your kid's father" he demanded.

"I d-don't know."

"This kid's tough. . . . Well, back to work on the old lady."

"No, please don't hurt her," Mimi blubbered. Her mouth quivered out of control as she saw the agony, the desperation of her mother's eyes. "I know who. It was Mr. Wilks. Isn't that who you want me to say?"

"If it's true. If you go downtown and swear to it. Monday."

"Yes. I promise. Don't hurt her again. I will. I swear!"

"We'll know quick if you don't, and you'll be sorry. We ain't been here. We're at a party. Witnesses. . . . C'mon, let's get back to that party before we're missed."

Two weeks later her mother was feeling well enough to walk around, but her air of intimidation was heartbreaking. They just couldn't cheer each other up. Whatever they talked about turned mournful.

"It's a shame about Tom Wilks losing his position," her mother sighed. "He never answered your letter, did he?"

Mimi shook her head. "I just have to make him talk to me. He's so hurt that he tried to walk right past me when I was waiting outside his apartment. I explained and explained. He listened and went on. Not a word."

"Try again, baby."

"I'll *try*."

He did at least let her come up.

When they were standing inside his apartment she tried to communicate with him wordlessly, but instead of understanding, he said, "I think the melting, tender young appeal of those large brown eyes is already established."

"You can't think I wanted to do such a thing to you. You can't not believe how they beat my mother and forced me to do what I did. It was the hardest thing I ever had to do. I cried every night about it. To betray the man I love was the worst. . . ."

He cut her off. "I know. You had no choice."

"You say it unforgivingly."

"You did try to do it another way, I admit. Tried to seduce me into marriage."

"You think I *knew?* You think I knew *then* that I was pregnant? Oh, I didn't. Honest to God. Say you *believe* me, Mr. Wilks."

"All right. But you *did* know you weren't a virgin. And you knew I assumed you were. At the very moment you were proclaiming your total, all-out selfless love . . . when you were presenting your whole life to me, when your great love should have compelled you to tell me the truth about yourself. . . ."

"I was ashamed. I felt dirty. It was rape, mass rape, Mr. Wilks."

"So I've heard. And I'm sorry about it. Believe me, very sorry. I can't do a thing about it."

"I don't expect . . ." she began.

He cut in. "The point is that there's no point for us. We can't be friends. I'm hunting a job and a new apartment. I want the tide to turn for you and your mother. I can't turn it. I want you to have some luck and happiness. But . . . well, we're not going to see each other again. This is it. This is goodbye."

She couldn't move. She looked at him in anguish, her eyes brimming.

"I won't say goodbye."

"You have to."

She nodded. She went over to the door. She stopped and just rested, her forehead on the door. Finally he came over, patted her shoulder.

"I'll walk you home, this once more."

✣ TEN ✣

BY JULY SHE HAD GROWN in all directions, especially outward in the stomach. Every time she looked at herself
sidewise in a mirror she giggled, just as she did when suddenly the little thing in there would kick or turn. Her
mother and Mrs. Cobb, the Welfare lady, were having the
baby with her.

They were as excited as she was. They read books and
articles about having and rearing babies and instructed
and pampered and tended her like a queen. They were
pleased about her health and glowing good spirits. They
wouldn't let her be scared. It seemed so easy, so delightful.
She was scared that she wasn't scared enough. She loved
fussing around with the layette and planning all the things
she would have to do for years and years ahead to the
time the little thing would be as old as she was. Sometimes
it was a boy, sometimes a girl. Her doctor was more than
satisfied with her general condition and state of mind.

Actually what the baby in her body had done for their
lives was a miracle. Once in awhile she let herself think
about the irony of such goodness springing from such
horror but the idea was distasteful and she almost succeeded in forgetting there was any connection between the
two things. The real experience that should have gone with
the inception of the baby was yet to come and there was
no doubt who would provide that experience. He was
somewhere in the world. They would find each other and
perform the mating act that would somehow establish him
physically as the father, as he was in her mind anyway.

She had had the excitement of false labor the last week
in June. Then again on July 4th. But on the 10th it was
real. The pains started about an hour apart. The time

span narrowed quickly and within twelve hours they were down to twenty-minute intervals. Her mother hurried back from phoning the doctor.

"It's to the hospital with you. He'll be there."

When the cab pulled out with them Mimi cried glee-fully:

"And away we go!"

"It's going to be easy for you, like it was with me."

"I know it. And you know something. . . ." She broke off, gripped her mother and held on as a sharper cramp caught her. "Whew!" she laughed when it released her. "I was *going* to say that the labor doesn't even hurt. And it doesn't even though it does and you know why? Because a thing that's necessary and has a purpose. . . . Whew! . . . . Ask the driver did he ever deliver a baby. You know what? I hope he has to . . ."

He didn't. They got her up to the labor room, and there was her doctor.

He joked, calling her by her initials:

"How's my fellow M.D.?"

"Ready, willing and . . . *Here we go!*"

The sac burst. They started her toward the delivery room.

"Not too much dope. I want to be in on it!"

She was on the delivery room table. Two nurses were there helping her. There was a sort of team spirit, a syn-chronization of her, the doctors' and nurses' efforts . . . squeeze and pressure . . . relax, panting a little, then an-other thrust. . . . She had a sense of high-pitch crisis, not dangerous. She wished there was some kind of overhead mirror so she could see, because she could feel the baby emerging.

The nurses were mopping sweat off her face and the doctor was holding the double handful of new life up on his palms for a moment. He carried it out of sight. She heard its piercing cry and lay grinning while her breast heaved almost like sympathetic crying with the little thing.

It was a girl, six pounds two ounces. Mrs. Cobb had the fantastic notion that she was beautiful, so did Mimi's mother.

"Well, Mimi, can't you choose a name?"

"I can't decide between Goofy. . . . Piglette. . . . Red-skin . . . or maybe . . . oh, Diane?"

"No. Really. No."

"Well, then, there's one I like best. Barbara. H'm?"

"Oh, yes. That's nice . . . Barbara . . ."

"Barbara Diane. . . . look! Look at that yawn . . . that mouth . . . that Grand Canyon *mouth.* . . ."

"You quit picking on that doll! Barbara. Barbara Diane."

She had visitors galore in the ward. All the other women made her a pet. Mrs. Cobb and her mother brought presents not only for the baby but for her. She was simply in bliss when the baby was brought in to nurse. Not from her breasts, but she held and cradled it to the warmth of her body while it was taking the bottle, so it would have the right *feel* about everything.

Truly Barbara Diane wasn't pretty. But when she came home, women from several apartments were out to have a look and they acted like she was beautiful.

In a few days Barbie started to look pale pink and soft instead of blistered. Her head was fuzzy and silly-round, and she had big, dumb blue eyes and the teensiest little fingers. The poor little thing cried a lot in the heat and got a rash. Then, frighteningly, she began to cough one night.

It got worse. Her mother called the doctor. The cough was horrible, croupy, and strangling. Mimi tried to hold her during the racking violence to absorb some of the strain on the tiny body. She thought she'd burst her blood vessels. Her breathing got ragged, and she couldn't be held. She had to be free. She was fighting for air. The sound was dreadful. The doctor got there. He gave her something that eased her breathing, but she cried piteously, weakly. The doctor decided to rush her to the hospital.

Mimi, carrying the baby, her mother, the doctor, were on the way downstairs to his car when Barbara's weak whimpering cry stopped. She gasped and kicked and waved her arms and her tiny hands clawed out twitchily and she started to choke and cough. Abruptly her round head lolled, motionless.

"Doctor!" Mimi shouted.

He swung around, took the baby, and blew in her mouth with his, several times. She began to breathe. He turned her upside down.

94

"Put the blanket on the floor. Then hold her like this . . . the way my hands are . . . that's it."

Mimi knelt, holding her. She still breathed. The doctor gave an injection. They went on to the car. In the car Barbie's heart stopped.

The doctor stabbed a needle through the chest directly into the heart with an adrenalin.

They drove on to the hospital. But Mimi knew she was holding a dead baby all the way.

Riding home in the doctor's car at four in the morning she lay on the back seat, just staring. She had no more tears. There was no pain in her breast, just an empty, hopeless emptiness. She kept thinking:

"What's the use? What's the use?"

✤ ELEVEN ✤

SHE WAS SIXTEEN NOW and hadn't seen Tom Wilks for a year. Almost by acident she overheard two girls in a bus mention his name and found out he taught in a private school on the upper west side. She went there and from across the street she saw him leave school one day.

She followed him distantly and after he'd entered a building she checked the mailboxes. There was his name and apartment number! Just seeing him and knowing where he lived and that he was well and had a position was enough. She didn't try to contact him.

But she kept thinking about him and going up to that neighborhood to catch glimpses of him. Always, afterward, she felt better. There was a magic about his mere name, and the actual sight of him was somehow like a stroking hand. She would stay away and think about him more than if she'd gone. Finally she just had to see him, even if he just said: "Go away."

She bathed and lotioned herself and brushed her hair until it was lustrous and dressed meticulously. She left home after dark and was at his building in a half hour. She rang the buzzer and he spoke over a building phone and she said who she was and he didn't send her away.

She went toward his second-floor door and wobbled with sudden lack of confidence although she had prepared herself to appeal to his every possible taste. For regal sophistication she'd upswept her hair and capped it with a hoop she'd covered with ribbons and lace; then her fleecy pink hip-length coat, flaring out in front as it did, gave her a bundled look like a contented young matron; her narrow skirt sirenishly defined her thighs and rounded thrust of her derriere; yet, her shoes were neat, unsexy flats and school-girlish, if that was the element in her he would like best to remember.

Tom Wilks opened the door and began suddenly to smile and Mimi, prepared to flinch, blossomed.

"Come in here! It's great to see you."

His hands came out, spanned her shoulders and he backstepped, drawing her in. She looked up at him, laughing. She puckered up as he bent and kissed her lips lightly.

"Mimi, you got prettier!"

"You, too!"

They laughed. It was as if the only interruption in their friendship had been the elimination of trouble. Soon they were sitting, asking, telling, leaning toward each other as they talked. He wanted to know about everything, everybody. She brought him up to date, making light of every trouble, passing it by quickly. Finally she said:

"Tom, I never could get it through my head that you didn't love me. I guess it was silly."

"In a sense, no, it wasn't, Mimi. In the very finest sense."

Mimi sighed. "It was deep, your love, and it was high. Exalted. Because of honor you refused to violate what you thought was my innocence. But that's past. Our baby has come and gone and. . . ."

"Our baby?" he interrupted quietly.

Mimi nodded. "Barbara Diane. Barbie. I loved her so much and she was taken from me so suddenly. . . . I'll never forget how I felt feeling her suffer and knowing I was life to her and she couldn't hold to me. I couldn't even comfort. . . ." she couldn't go on. She didn't cry but she couldn't speak and she just stared hollowly. She was aware of his good, warm hands, his soothing voice. He went and got her a glass of wine. She drank.

"Ah," she said, smiling. "Thanks. I guess I ought to explain why I said 'our baby,' so you won't think I'm, well . . ." she made a trailing gesture ". . . crazy. In my heart, all through the pregnancy you were the father. I always had a dream that after the baby was born and my figure got better you would make love to me and complete the situation. Even though, physically the act of love would be after, instead of before, the baby. Do you know what I mean? Tom, do you see how I need to have my baby's birth connected with a love experience instead of a

97

hate experience? Physically it doesn't make sense, but . . . well."

"You poor kid. I understand very well how you could have felt that way."

"I still do, Tom. I came here to make a proposition. Marriage isn't in your plans. But the need for a woman is. Let me be the one. I want to be your mistress."

He stood up and walked away. He came back and looked at her in distress.

"I can't!" he blurted. "I'm unable. Sexually. I *can't* love you that way."

"Tom, *no*. My poor dearest, you're not CRIPPLED?"

"Not that," he said tightly. "I can't make love to you, that's all."

He lit a smoke and flopped into a chair. Mimi sighed, relieved, then smiled to herself. She went over and casually slipped onto his lap.

"Let me stay here and talk to you. I never realized how true it is that women are more realistic than men. Sweetheart, you're an idealist. You have rejected sex. Of course I know a million reasons why that's the finest thing to do. But sex itself isn't a low thing. Tom, it stands to reason, doesn't it, when sex is God's method for creating life and the human race that it is good. A part of love. Even if it gets filthied by ugly elements, by itself it isn't a thing to be rejected." She took his face in her hands, petting his cheeks, and kissed his lips. "Wasn't that nice? You like my kisses and my body. Don't you see how pleasant it is just touching each other?" She began to grin slyly. She could feel his definite male response. She whispered in his ear. "See? See how much you like my sitting on your lap? Oh, it makes me so happy." She kissed him. "And I'll make you happy. Love me, Tom, love me!"

He shook his head. "Get up," he ordered. He boosted her off his lap, stood up himself. "I've got to confess something. It's you or me. Going on believing in and loving me could break you, Mimi. Instead, I'll break me. The picture of me that exists in your mind. I'm a homosexual. A pansy. Fairy. Queer."

She looked at him, stunned. She reddened. "I think that's cheap," she said angrily. "Cowardly. Dishonest. Unworthy of you. Be man enough to just say, 'Mimi, I don't care for you, forget me, beat it'. . . . Well," she

98

shrugged, "you tried that, and here I came back like an albatross around your neck. So I suppose the only other ways of getting rid of me would be to beat me up or disgust me, then I'll be cured of you. Well, I'm not cured or disgusted. I've seen pansies and know what they look like. You're the most unconvincing imitation I ever saw. Anyway, your message is clear. Goodbye. Where's my damned coat?"

"Of course you refuse to accept it, but sit down and hear me out."

Dumbly, feeling vaguely sick, she sat and listened intently.

"As a kid I lived in a tough neighborhood. I was like you. Serious. Musical. Played the violin. Studied hard. The toughs resented me. Ganged me. Beat me up, smashed my fiddle, stole my lunch money. I fought back and hated them. But it was either get beat up every day or join them. I couldn't stay out.

"In the gang it wasn't much better. The bigger ones kicked the little ones around. Toughening us. I could only whip a few. Most of them could whip me, and did. I took it so hard they made me special and worked me over and over and never stopped till I was crawling and begging for mercy. I got bigger, learned to use weapons . . . knives, clubs, bottles, bricks, hooks, knuckles, chains, you name it. I got mean and tough on one level . . . Physically. But before that they broke all my sense of manhood.

"The girls in the auxiliary went only for the toughest. When I tried anything they laughed at me. One time, one of them . . . a wild little beauty, she was just plain fire . . . felt sorry for me. She belonged to the leader, but I went to a room with her. I started kissing her; she kissed me. She slipped off her clothes and I took off mine. She saw I was well made and said: 'What a man!' admiringly. And that was it . . . All my passion vanished. I tried to make love; she tried to help me. I wasn't capable. In my mind I knew she really belonged to a better man, that I wasn't a man at all, that I was a crawling vile, low slave who had to yield to real men . . ."

He became pale and red in turn. He didn't see her, his eyes were bright and fierce and looking into a horror chamber in the past. He went out of the room; she heard him in the kitchen, getting a drink.

99

"Bring me one too," she called. "A liquor drink."

He brought back two highballs. He sat on the couch, she in her chair. They drank and sat, not looking at each other, sipped again.

"Well, if you've had a rest," he said, "I'll go on. Of course I got older, stronger, more confident. Underneath, though . . . well, something was broken in me. I found out in a dozen cases. I adore beautiful girls; they stir me; I enjoy the sight and sound and movement and gestures and manners and shapes of them; I want to embrace and cherish and enjoy them.

"I used to court them and the time would come when I'd try to make love. Something in me would know I was an imposter, that I had no right to assume the function of a true man, that I was sham, that the woman in her instinct would sense it. . . . would scorn me, would lash me with her contempt, would broadcast to her friends and mine the real truth about me.

"It got so I was only at ease with men and boys. Those who seemed less than men than I. One time I felt so sorry for one of them that . . . well, no details, but I was happy with him. On and off that passion assails me like an insanity. Most of the time I'm like a man with a hangover who can't bear the thought of liquor. Then abruptly, the craving comes. . . ."

"And you yield to it?"

"You don't understand!" he cried. "When your will and spirit are broken you can't resist; you have nothing to fight with. You don't know how deeply it kills you. You lose your power, your confidence. You turn your own hate and contempt against yourself and become weak, loathsome to yourself; defeated. . . ."

"But you still *want* girls, don't you?"

"I'm afraid to want them, and fail again. But yes, yes, more than anything under God's sun I want them. . . ."

"Me?"

"You."

Mimi finished her drink. She got up and went over for her purse. "Can I use your bathroom?"

He led her to it. At the door she said: "When I come out I'll be naked . . . you be, too."

"Mimi, you don't understand how horrible it is for a man to fail . . . I'm . . ." His face looked drawn, his eyes

100

were jumpy. She gazed up at him, then put her hand gently on his face.

"With me," she said softly, "if you failed it would be all right. But with me you won't. I *know*."

He kissed her mouth. "My God, but I want you, Mimi. I think you're right. With you . . . *yes* . . . It'll be right . . . The way you love me . . . and I love you, too. . . . Don't be long, Mimi!"

She undressed slowly, carefully. She studied her breasts, her belly, hips, legs, feet, toenail polish, fingernail polish and finally gravely, her face, praying that there would be no failure of her desirability. She decided to unpin her hair and she was glad she had because when she stirred it out silkily around her cheeks and shoulders, it gave her a soft, sleepy, slow look.

Nothing would be rushed or tense or pressured, and he would know that failure with her would be no shame and would not affect her love. But Mimi knew he would not only be able to make love to her, but that something above and beyond them, a finger of Fate had given her this mission in life, to heal and restore and enrich and save this man.

She wasn't prepared for the sight of him, sitting nearly naked in white shorts on the edge of the bed, nor for exposing her own nakedness. Automatically she put a hand and forearm acorss her breasts, concealed herself below. She moved lightly on the balls of her bare feet, drawing the arches into taut, lovely lines. Against the dimness of the bedroom the paleness of her bare skin seemed touched with moonglow. The shadows flickered delicately over her slim, gracefully moving legs. Her breasts were fuller and very firm, their lower curves jutting upward, the pink nipples uptilted.

Tom waited, seated, staring at her, his mouth parted a little as if he was already panting and excited. She moved to the edge of his knees and stood facing him, and removed her arm from her breasts and dropped her other and let her thin arms hang motionless.

He reached out and his lightly grazing fingers brushed along the satiny expanse of skin at the side of her hips, and the sensation was so exquisite that she drew her legs together, lifting and bending one knee. She joggled the point of her knee against his, and stepped in between his

101

knees, and both his hands spanned her hips, caressing very slowly up and down, and she put her hands on his face and bent down to him, her hair falling past her cheeks onto his.

She kissed his mouth, holding the kiss a long time. Then she just stood and gazed at him while he glided his hands over her body, touched her breasts. She pushed one shoulder forward so that her breast touched his face.

When he kissed her breast her heart began to hammer and her senses giddied. She seized his head and mashed his face up against her body and he kissed her breasts several times. Then, lifting and pulling, he drew her on top of him and lay down. He turned her on her side and kissed her mouth and stroked, and she stroked his bared upper back, feeling the nervous play of muscle under his skin. He drew one of her legs between his, and his hand at her back pressed her forward, packing her in to him. He had began to pant, and there was no doubt of the rousing of his whole body.

She felt him get up on his hands and knees and she lay on her back, and closed her eyes, and she could feel the beginning delightful little clutching spasms of desire in her lower stomach. She rubbed her hand against the hair on his chest, and then glided her arms up and around as he came into position to cover her. She was open and waiting, and he was lifting her and he was coming closer and closer, and then . . . and then. . . .

The fever seemed to leave him suddenly the instant he made contact. He swore in a low, hoarse voice and flung himself onto his side beside her. Mimi didn't say anything. After awhile he began again to kiss her body and her mouth and to stroke her. He came again to passion. His very flesh gave off heat and he panted. With a rush he almost flung himself on her again.

The same thing happened.

Tom got off the bed. He lit a cigarette. He came and stood looking down at her. She reached up and squeezed his hand, smiling tenderly.

"Have another drink. Then we'll just lay together. It'll be all right next time."

"Yes!"

He went out and got a drink and came back. For almost

an hour they lay together afterward. He made love with his hands, with his kisses, with endearing words. She responded and tried every way of seduction she could think of. But he did not become roused again. At last they both got up and dressed.

They just said words to each other when she was leaving the apartment. They didn't look at each other.

She was so nervous and fatigued and sick at her stomach and headachy she didn't know how she made it home. She came down with a bad cold that hung on for several days.

The situation between her and her mother was turning into a mockery. Her mother went out, Mimi didn't know where, several times a week, often coming back late—and drunk. She was coarsening too, starting to lose her looks.

Mimi never asked her anything any more, or told her anything either. If she herself had ever found anybody she wanted to stay out all night with she'd have done it. She came and went on the street without fear because she had a little secret for anybody who might bother her. It was a knife strapped to her thigh. She kept wishing she'd have occasion to use it.

It was a beautiful knife, with a flat, taped handle and a gleaming seven-inch blade that came to a needle point. Both edges were razor sharp. She killed lots of lonely time sharpening it with a whetstone.

One night she'd gone to a double feature in the neighborhood when she caught sight of a handsome boy in a suit. When she saw his full face she sneered. It was Doc. He was by himself. He came and sat behind her in the movie. She moved. He moved too. Moving again, she said: "I'll call the manager," and he let her alone then.

As Mimi walked home Doc stepped suddenly out of a doorway and grabbed her. He pulled her into the building and rushed her to the basement. She didn't yell or struggle very hard. She even went into a storage room with him. He switched on a dim bulb revealing a table and cot, and shut the door. Mimi cowered, watched him tremblingly.

"This time, Mimi, sweetie, you won't be scared."

He took her around the waist and tried to kiss her. She turned her face away a couple of times, then she sighed and let him kiss her.

103

Freeing himself, he grinned. "I'm the Doc with the medicine you want, baby." He laced his fingers in hers, bent her hand back sharply.

Mimi winced. "Don't hurt me," she said meekly.

"You mean 'please!' "

"Please."

"Lay down and pull up your dress."

She sat down on the cot. She pulled her skirt up a little, showing some of her legs and smiled sweetly. "You can see a little, first. Then turn out the light. Please?"

When he reached for the light Mimi hiked her skirt all the way up. She slipped off the knife binding. When he came to the cot she had the knife out. Clenching the handle she drew back her arm, then aimed at his lower stomach and drove the blade as hard as she could.

He yelled and fell back and she stabbed again. He fell to the floor. Mimi turned on the light and grinned down at him, lying there clutching his lower stomach with his bloody hands. His face was white, his eyes had a shocked, panicky look. He writhed and rocked himself trying to hold in the pain. He jabbered and blubbered, begging for help. Mimi just grinned and wiped the knife on his coat. A fiery, exultant sensation raced through her. She pulled her dress up to her hip, casually fastened the knife to her thigh. She sneered, spat in his face and walked out.

She went outside and waited. When he came out half-crawling, she laughed out loud, swished her behind and walked on ahead of him.

Her exultance wouldn't die down. She had to share it with somebody, and even though there was nobody really, including Tom, she went to him.

He listened to her pour the whole story out gleefully.

"He was in agony. What a bang! I know what I'm going to do, darling," she enthused. "Get the rest of them! Spud, Rocky, Dopey. Every one of them. One by one. Track them down. Kill or half-kill them. So they crawl! Vengeance is *sweet!*" She smacked her lips. "Lover, lover, I'm fiery. Let's try once more!"

"No. Listen to me, Mimi!"

"Don't advise me to drop the revenge!"

"It could turn you ugly. Make you the female equivalent of them. A bitch. Think about it!"

"*You* think about it, and *you* save me from it. Give me

something better. Come back from your queerhood and take care of me! *Then* I'll promise! Have you got the guts for another try on that bed? And if we fail this time I'll quit. It'll be goodbye for real. Then you wouldn't have to feel guilty or ashamed. You'll be free like my mother wants to be to go to hell. She in her way. You in yours. Me in mine . . ." Suddenly she started to cry. "Don't let me turn that way, Tom. I'll save you. You save me. I can't get over loving you. I just CAN'T!"

That night and two other times he took her to bed and did all he was capable of doing—nothing.

They both realized that any further relationship would turn them into enemies, so they broke off completely.

✤ TWELVE ✤

AT NINETEEN Mimi was a beauty. She was inches taller and her fuller figure was a striking blend of long graceful tapers and voluptuous surgings. The process of growth had subtly firmed and drawn out the roundings of her soft oval face giving her features greater delicacy. Sometimes spontaneously, her eyes revealed an earlier shining, wide-open very-young quality; more often she brought that appeal consciously into play.

At work in a steno pool at national headquarters offices of Drayton-Blieling Products Inc. she maintained a vaguely baffled, helpless air which pleased and flattered those executives she sometimes needed to turn to for guidance and advice. Among her co-workers, two of whom she roomed with, she let it be known that before taking this first job out in the big world, she'd had an unusually sheltered life.

The junior executives fished the steno pool all the time and she'd dated ten or twelve of them during her eight months at D-B. She had firmly established a reputation as a sweet green kid who couldn't be kissed before the third date and who stopped all handies games before they got started.

She didn't feel false in her pose of innocence since it was the basic truth about her and the character she was entitled to and would have had if her father hadn't died. Some of the girls thought she was stupid with her looks to be pecking away at a typewriter. But beauty was common-place in glamor careers. At D-B she stood out. Besides, even if she'd had talent for modelling or acting, such worlds were unstable. Her ambitions were: Security first.

Uneventful living. A nice small home on a quiet street. Last and least, a husband.

On a balmy Friday evening in early April, three years since she'd seen Tom Wilks, Mimi was strolling down Fifth with Jock Standish, one of the young bosses at D-B. He was taking her to "Hip Hip HEY," the hit musical at the Winter Garden.

Jock was one of her two top matrimonial prospects. On the emotional level he was her first choice. They were early and they moved languorously. As usual Jock was fascinatingly talkative. His range of knowledge was impressive on the impersonal level. Personally he swung between complaints and enthusiasms. D-B was his third job and he believed he was under-valued and held down and he was restless in the job. Within two short blocks he outlined four different new careers for himself and they all sounded possible.

He'd been a mathematical child prodigy, even touring to perform incredible wizardries. Suddenly, in his early teens, that genius in him had vanished. It had left him feeling like a plucked peacock. All his worked-for later achievements seemed empty and he sometimes felt his whole life would be a useless trying to catch up with himself. He was considered brilliant at D-B, but as everyone observed, he was erratic, sometimes dropping into grouchy, inert to-hell-with-everything slumps. And while he might skyrocket to become the youngest chairman of the board he might just as easily end in the gutter.

Walking with him in her special-for-the-occasion bouffant hairdo which spread fatly out from her cheeks her face seemed smaller, softer than usual. With Jock she had a sort of instinct for diminishing and subordinating herself, and a certain sense of rightness about being with him. He was tall, square-faced and handsome even when he scowled, which he did as often as he smiled. There was a vitality and underlying even his doubts, a vibrant confidence about him which soothed her.

He had a vaguely definable something . . . authority or initiative or whatever . . . which "carried" her. He gave her an easy sense of her own attractiveness and she knew she looked nice in the pearl gray jacket and the short midnight blue taffeta evening frock. The flaring knee-length skirt swung like a lazy, whispering bell around

107

her sleek nylon-sheathed legs and there was an elegant lift to her feet in her smart black suede high-heel pumps. Jock looked down at her legs and said:

"To prove what a smart kid I was: Once in a backyard a girl was standing with her legs apart and I dropped a mirror on the ground between her feet."

"You know you're not to talk to me that way." She smiled at him.

"Don't you know you don't need to overplay with me, Mimi? Oh, I know you're an authentic virgin . . . a pity . . . but what kind of fishermen are you going to hook with the stupidity bit you pull at the office?"

"You're not so bad. What makes you think the stupidity's a 'bit'?"

"I don't think it. I know. And you're better than that. Cunning in the long run never pays off. At least not in Sincereville. That's where a girl's got to live. A girl like you, Mimi. Fakeville, you can't live there."

She looked up at him with calm, steady eyes, her lips pursed slightly. Though he didn't actually look like Tom Wilks, the breadth of his forehead, the clear, serious eyes, the good mouth had the same high quality.

"You're the Sincereville gentleman who dates a girl on a week day so that her work day plus the long evening will weaken her resistance."

"I told you. A sportsman warning small game."

"Small game." Her smile froze.

"Small game. I could have knocked you off like that. Just offered the asking price. Marriage. The trouble is I've got the price. The true desire to marry the true you."

"Don't lecture me. I don't want to marry you."

"I need marriage. It'll settle me down. Make me content and resigned."

"Don't be the cute boy wonder. I don't *want* to marry you," she said angrily. "I'm not interested in your medical problem that you think marriage will cure. You're insulting."

"I'm not getting through. I mean, Mimi, some of my natural intensity that should be going into my job is sidetracked. . . ." She was astonished to see that his eyes were fixed on her burningly. "Sidetracked onto you. I want you. I actually think I'm in love with you. I mean I *am.*"

108

She stopped close to a building and looked at him wonderingly.

"How can I be mad at you? A thing like that touches a girl," she said smiling softly.

"Don't generalize. Does it touch you?"

He peered narrowly at her. She gazed calmly at him.

"I said it touches a girl. I'm a girl."

"But," he persisted, "it doesn't touch *you*."

"You appeal to me," Mimi said patiently. "I could learn to love you. That's why this is our last date. If I married you and started to love you it would betray something . . . somebody. Never mind who. You don't know him. Next to him you're the person I care most about. But if it came about that you became *first* in my heart I would hate you."

"Jesus, you're as screwed up as I am."

"Well, it's clear to me. I'm who counts with me. Do you still want to take me to the show?"

"Why, of course, Mimi. Who's to get the goodies? Mr. Double-Negative, eh? What if I warned him about you?"

"I know you wouldn't."

"Not to do him a favor. But the *idea* of *you* being owned by him could make me stop it. But that would assume I still felt you were something precious and desirable and fine and adorable and worth trying to hold." He stopped. He looked at her with vast scorn. "I misjudged you. You're a bum. So go right ahead, I'd never spill." He opened his wallet, pulled out the theater ticket envelope. He gave her one of the tickets. The other he tore up. He looked at her grimly then turned his back, walked away. Scowling, Mimi went on and enjoyed the show.

She enjoyed the same show next night with Randy Partch. A medium tall, narrowly made man of about thirty, Randy was not-unintelligent, not-incompetent, not-unhandsome. A Mr. Double-Negative in a way, but in another way his lack of strong positive traits meant balance and stability. Though he wasn't likely to soar to the top, he wouldn't fall either. He had solid ability and he would plod up to a reasonably high plateau and provide a comfortable, emotionally undemanding life.

As a wife, she would conscientiously keep house, provide good meals, maintain order and provide a certain amount of pleasure. She was pretty and young and she would be bringing into the marriage everything but the one thing she didn't have to give . . . love. In some countries that kind of marriage was considered best since passions were disruptive.

"Hip Hip HEY!" was fast and bouncy with brassy music, witty sex, luscious girls in exuberant songs and jazzy dances. Mimi's favorite scene was wild with skimpily costumed cavegirls walloping, conquering and dragging off the males.

Beside her Randy Partch, whose laughter was usually a gargling sound, fairly yelped with joy. He kept glancing to see if Mimi was appreciating it. When the men reappeared, happily tamed, Mimi was imagining that the girls had emasculated them offstage. Her teeth were clenched under a soft smile, as she thought about the Rustlers and wished Tom Wilks hadn't argued her out of stalking and knifing them all. She'd turned bitchy anyway or she wouldn't be here with Randy Partch. She reached over and pressed his hand.

After the show she let him urge a second and finally a third champagne cocktail on her. Going out to the cab she'd emboldened him by displaying a slack half-silly grin and muzzy eyes. It was their tenth date and on the past four she'd allowed increasingly friendlier good-night kisses. So in the cab she didn't protest his first kiss till it became fervent. Then, with a kind of automatic nice-girl reflex, Mimi stiffened and pushed him away. She stared, wide eyed.

"You mustn't, Randy," she pleaded, barely aloud, as if too weak to do much more than move her softly parted lips tremulously.

"Mimi," he said huskily. "Mimi!"

His eyes probed. She showed him defenselessness. He doubled the assault, not only mashing his mouth into the red-ripe yieldingness of her lips but inserting his hand between her coat and the breastfront of her dress. She whimpered faintly, seized his wrist and pulled, her whole body squirming. She rolled her face, gasped for air, and said catchingly:

"You're so strong . . . you mustn't. . . ."

He was kissing her again. While his hand performed under her coat, alternately massaging and pinching lightly,

110

her hand loosened on his wrist. Presently her encircling fingers embraced, then caressed delicately. She gave a faint lurch as if one final wave of resistance was running through and out of her body, then, with the faintest of moans audible only to her and his own ears, she lay passively surrendered, her head on the seatback under his, her fluttery eyelids quietly closed in bliss.

While she was thus being made a passion slave by Randy Partch, Mimi was visualizing chalked numbers on a blackboard and multiplying $3,500 by 43. It would be forty-three years till she was 62 and on Social Security, and at her present salary, she would have earned by then . . . $150,500. She re-computed. Check. $150,500. Which would be earning it the hard way.

There was an easy way. Permit little Randy to over-exert himself for a few minutes while she endured effortlessly. Then she would descend from the fever of ecstasy, realize her shame, cover her face and wet her cheeks and weep the weeps of lost innocence. And unless she had miscalculated his basic tameness he would propose.

If sterner measures were needed Mimi was not for nothing the 19-year-old daughter of a 26-year-old redhead calling herself Dinny Danser who was currently in Florida or France or someplace with an ancient millioniare. She'd give Randy a taste of all-out hysteria shot through with dainty little threats to spread the news of his lecherous conduct around the office.

Randy had a reputation in his job and the hope of a lifetime career at D-B. If it became known he'd betrayed a sweet, green kid there might be serious reconsideration of his integrity and sense of responsibility by his superiors. Especially the ones who most wanted to take her to bed themselves.

The cab stopped. He searched his pockets for money as if plagued by fleas, all the while casting nervous glances at her for signs that she might be emerging from the passion drugged state he had her in. She stayed captive, let herself be led inside like a zombie. He rushed her into the self-service elevator like a man pursued. His narrow body squirmed under the bulky, open overcoat; his scarf and maroon tie were awry, his hat set at a wobbly angle.

Sometimes lust gave luster; in Randy it brought out pink splotches. His features tightened till his face seemed to come to a point like a snout and there was something furtively unpleasant about his nervousness.

As the elevator went up and she became aware of herself confined alone with him her eyes widened and she said in a panic not entirely feigned:

"Randy, I'm scared. If I go up for a minute, promise you won't kiss me. . . ."

He kissed her at once, and she let her resistance dissolve. Inside his apartment she stood looking flustered and pawing futilely at his hands as he removed her coat. He kissed her neck from behind. She tightened her shoulders and doubled her fists and stood rigid as if withstanding too much bliss.

"Trust me, darling," he said shakily. "You know I love you. You gorgeous, adorable thing. You're beautiful."

She dropped her lashes shyly. "I'm just pretty."

"Beautiful!"

"I want to go home."

"No, sweetheart, you know you don't want to go home."

"I never was alone in a man's apartment. I know what you're going to do to me. I won't let you." He kissed her throat, her ears, his hands moved over her breasts and body. "Please! Don't make me get in trouble. I WANT to get in trouble," she said suddenly, passionately. She pressed her mouth to his. She broke away, leaned her head on his shoulder, panting. "Can't you see how bad I want to. . . . Don't let me, Randy. I've got no character. Take me home! Don't let me be bad. It's so hard, so hard, to be good . . . Randy. . . ."

He carried her into his bedroom. As Randy was kneeling at bedside taking off her high-heeled shoes and kissing her knees she smiled twistedly. She thought: "All right, Tom? See me? I'm *worse* than you could ever *possibly* be, darling."

Randy came on the bed and unzipped the back of her dress and kissed her all the way down to the waist. He took off her bra. She stood up and let her dress slide to the floor. She looked down coolly with a sense of command as he crouched down to take off her panties, his face pressing feverishly to her stomach, her thighs, kissing her and panting.

She lay on the bed and allowed him to work out his

112

little fever. When he hopped up off the bed Mimi lay there waiting for the proper moment to start the weeps. It took her a long time. Finally she knew she didn't have the stamina for the long haul with a creature like this. She sat up and began to dress. She went into the bathroom. When she came out he was having a drink and a smoke. They smiled at each other.

"I really must get home."

"Of course. Of course, Mimi," he said, loudly not proposing.

✤ THIRTEEN ✤

THE WEEKEND, the week, the next weekend went by without either Randy or Jock asking for another date. They weren't among the bosses who called her out of the pool for added dictation. Mimi had invitations from several other men and declined them all. Evenings she watched TV, read magazines, attended to her clothes and toilette. Time was filled, but dilutedly. Her roommates bored her with advice every time a "good prospect" phoned her for a date.

Thursday at work Jock Standish came to the end of his fuse, blew up and resigned. He looked happy about it. When he said goodbye to her in the office he spoke lightly and affectionately. Afterward Mimi was surprisingly let down. She'd not only counted on a reconciliation . . . she'd somehow looked on Jock as Tom Wilks' successor.

Thursday evening she found in the mailbox at her apartment a funny postcard from her mother in New Orleans. It made her mad, then lonesome, finally depressed.

She set out walking nowhere. She window shopped in midtown, dropped into record shops, sat awhile in the main library reading room. She walked again, stopping twice in cafeterias, once for coffee and sandwich, once for dessert. Naturally she thought about Tom Wilks. She didn't connect him with what he said he was; she didn't understand how he could be that; she could not imagine it, but it was a fact that must be accepted and she had no conscious intention of seeking him out.

Even when she realized she was in his neighborhood she didn't expect nor really want to see him. Mimi turned along his street and entered his building only to see if he still lived there. She read his badly smudged name-card, THOMAS R. WILKS, forlornly. Leaving the building she saw again that his place was dark and went idly down the block. She wished they could live sexlessly together, going their own ways, but having talks and walks and meals together. . . . Mimi sighed.

Abruptly she saw him coming out of the subway. Not alone. Not with a girl. But with a . . . a creature.

She'd never really seen . . . or anyway understood . . . Tom's actual connection with . . . with homosexuality and it was like ripping away a final shred of hope that he had really been lying. Her face colored. She turned and hurried away almost frenziedly, so he wouldn't see her and know she had seen his shame with her own eyes. After a few steps she felt like she was fleeing. Her lips mashed together and her eyes flashed. She stopped, did an almost military about-face and began to follow them.

With rising agitation she watched the imitation woman in man's clothes swishing along beside Tom, gazing up across its shoulder at him. Mimi understood the love that that homosexual must feel for Tom's manly beauty. The passion Tom would rouse in anyone was easy to understand. But to understand all was NOT to forgive all. She clenched teeth. When they entered the building she wasn't far behind. She came up stamping every step with her high heels. They were opening the door to go in. Mimi stabbed a forefinger toward them and yelled:

"YOU! Don't you go in there!"

The pair of them gaped at her. She ran forward, her face squinched, her eyes fixed with pure female fury on the man who wanted to love her man. When the homosexual sensed her purpose he caught at Tom's arm. Mimi leaped, grabbed his arm and flung it downward.

"Don't you touch him. Get out!" She slapped his face with her free hand, hit him from the other side with her purse. She grabbed his jacket front and bracing her feet she backstepped, pulling him. He shut his eyes and began to squeal like a pig, not raising a hand to defend himself. She yanked him along to the stairs. "Get down there." She kicked him. "Don't ever come back or I'll tear your eyes out! Get me? Beat it!"

He was only too glad to get away from the mad female

115

creature. Fuming, she advanced on Tom's apartment. Tom grinned.

"Saved in the nick of time."

"Don't be funny and don't be blocking me. I'm coming in."

He stepped aside, mock-bowing.

"Fear not to enter. For here, Mimi, my beauteous, is sanctuary for the female virtu-ous."

"If you defend him I'll claw and kick you. Oh darling, darling Tom."

Mimi rushed to him and pulled his face down to her mouth and kissed him. She kissed him hard and fast. In a moment he put his arms around her and took over the kissing.

He withdrew. "Whew!" He flung his hat on a chair, loosened his tie. He looked at her, shaking his head. "What a morsel! Tell me, Mimi, tell me what good did I offend? Hell, Tantalus had it good compared with the torture you bring into my life." He began blithely, ended grimly. He walked angrily away, lit a cigarette shakily. "Maybe it's prejudice that I think you're the most exquisitely beautiful creature in this world . . . maybe it's unattainability."

He came and stood toweringly over her . . . an instant later he dropped to his knees before her, gripped her hands and stared up with a terrible expression and said in a guttural voice: "What are you? Why do you come here, tormenting me? You don't love me. You *hate* me." He got up, clenching his fists, paced away, back to her.

Mimi said levelly: "Tom, no more nonsense between us. You've got an operating sex instinct. You're going to use it in the way you want to. With me. Tom, we're not going to go on being beaten people deprived of what we've got coming from life. I've got you. You me."

She went directly to the bedroom. She was in the process of undressing when he came in. She sat on the bed and he sat beside her and it didn't take him long to become roused. Neither of them bothered to fully undress. In two minutes she was beneath him and he was passionate and starting to truly claim her as his woman when. . . .

She was off the bed like a scalded cat.

"Again! Again!" She stood with her stockinged feet

116

braced apart, her toes moving. She pushed back her blonde hair and thrust her face and upper body aggressively toward him.

"You're a yellow quitter. You don't have pride or dignity. No wonder you were always afraid women would see you were a sham and an imposter. You are. Not an imposter as a man but as a *human* being. I'm rightfully yours. You want me but you're too subhuman yellow prideless to make a REAL try. You don't say, 'I will. . . . I *will* take my woman. I won't, I won't stay beaten for life. . . .'"

"Don't give me that 'I will, I will, I won't, I won't.' A man who's been as profoundly scarred as I have can't, by blustering exhortations. . . ."

"You think because you were abused you can sit nursing yourself, and taking it out on life. Go ahead. You do worse to me than those trash rapists. You cut me deeper. And you know it. You said do *I* hate *you*. What a sneaky twist. In your instinct you know you're hurting me in the cruelest way you can. But you just go on and feel abused and innocent so you can ENJOY my suffering . . ."

He hit her so hard her ears rang. She fell, bouncing on one hip and jumped up. "See, it comes out. You like hurting me. That's not homosexual, that's sadistic. That's what you are—a sadist—no matter how you keep it hidden from yourself."

"You're making me furious, Mimi!"

"Good! Knock me down some more. Big man. If that's the best way you can express manhood with a woman it's a good thing you're not man enough to be around them."

He grabbed out with both hands, catching her belt in one, her skirt in the other. He hauled her to the bed, flung her on her back, and hovered over her, his face drawn and threatening.

"Don't talk like that to me. Understand? I could kill you for it."

"I wish the hell you would. As fast and painlessly as possible."

"That's a lie."

"Two weeks ago I let a ratty thing get on top of me and chug like a steam engine. That's the kind of thing I have

117

to belong to . . . because it's got that one little talent, and can take me to an altar where I'll vow vows and I'll belong to a thing like that simply because the man I love won't claim me. CAN'T claim me," she said nastily. She gathered spit. "I'm going to spit up in your face I despise you so much."

"O.K."

"Well, I can't. But I despise you."

"Mimi, don't. . . . You know you love me. I love you. Don't yank that away from me. . . ."

"I scorn you."

He began to kiss her greedily. She only endured it. Abruptly he cursed her. "You bitch, you dirty little bitch. . . . I could kill you. I love you so goddamned much . . . I . . ." He made a lightning gesture toward his lower body. She realized he'd opened his pants. He was on her, his whole body gripped by a rage and a fiery passion. . . .

Mimi hung there unalive, unbreathing, suspended in eternity.

He was touching her intimately. He was pressing against her. She stared up into his twisted face, waiting in a kind of terror, willing potency into him.

"Oh, Tom, don't stop!"

Her whole breath came out on a long, quivering moan. He was loving her!

His flesh in her flesh was fierce and pure and commanding and joy and exaltation flooded her and she was alive, gloriously gloriously alive at last. Never, never had there been an ecstasy like this. It went on and on and then it was burstingly finished and she just lay there laughing and crying and when he rolled away she turned with him, clinging to him and beginning to kiss him.

He said:

"It happened!"

"Yes! Yes!"

He sat up. He stood up. "But I mean, it HAPPENED!" He came back to her and crouched over her on his hands and knees, gazing down at her. "I love you, darling. I adore you. My God, do you REALIZE?"

"Yes."

"You can't go."

118

"Never. It's got to happen again. How long?"

"An hour. A half. Fifteen minutes."

"Maybe even sooner," she said seductively and began to caress him. He lowered himself beside her and they caressed one another. It happened again, much sooner!

She stayed the night. She woke once with a passionate yearning for him, not untouched by panic, and began to caress him. He woke hungry for her and possessed her at once. Later he was the one who woke her, as though he, too, must again test the new magic.

Neither of them went to work next day. They didn't even leave the apartment. They bathed together and they made love and they ate and talked and laughed and listened to records.

In particular, he played a jewel of a Chopin Etude, Opus 28, No. 4, several times and in front of him she freely and painlessly and unembarrassedly cried over the music.

At night they went out for dinner. They went to a movie and walked out, wanting each other undistractedly and compulsively. He borrowed a car Saturday and they went for a long ride out on Long Island. They stopped overnight in a wonderful motel beside the sea and enjoyed it so much they spent all day Sunday and another night.

They didn't make sexual love either night; it was no longer a compulsive problem and their simple being together was a lovemaking in itself. They didn't even discuss the mundane wheres and whens of formal marriage since they belonged together forever and she thought about the poem, *Annabel Lee*, and about a hundred other poems and lyrical music and she knew her old love, music, would again soon be part of their lives.

Because they knew the separation was temporary, just till the end of his teaching semester, they continued living at their places when they returned to the city. They were together nearly every evening, parting early on week nights. Weekends she stayed overnight.

Except one weekend. He phoned her Friday afternoon at work, explained regretfully that he'd been invited to his department head's suburban home to consult on the next year's teaching program. Several teachers were going, and she clearly understood it was a non-social affair.

119

She didn't think anything about it till the middle of the night. She woke with an uneasy sensation, a Shakespeare line flashing into her mind. "He doth protest too much. . . ." Tom's explanation *had* been elaborate. But why wouldn't he have wanted to assure her, convince her? She went back to sleep.

But Monday night when she complained about missing him, Tom became defensive and angry. When she wanted to go to his apartment he avoided it.

"You're all right, aren't you?" Mimi asked in a hushed voice while they were having coffees in a cafeteria. "I mean. . . ."

"Oh, for God's sake. Even normal males don't quite spend a full 24-hours a day every day making love. Tomorrow evening we will."

"We can't. I'm just before my period . . . maybe that's why I'm this way. I didn't mean to doubt you. I love you."

"I know. I love you, too. Keep remembering it!"

At work she was new and bright and obviously carrying a vast sweetness around in her breast. Everyone knew she was in love and asked many questions and got no answers. In the intervening weeks she and Tom faced routine details of the future which, with him, were fun.

He broke evening dates with her twice. After the second time she was worried and knew something was on his mind. She wished she hadn't prodded him. Something sordid that she'd never considered came out and made her feel as if she'd pushed her face into a wet spiderweb.

"Try to understand something, sweetheart," he said anxiously, looking tenderly at her. "I lived in a dirty half-world. People in it are vulnerable to something . . . blackmail. They get things on you . . . they're in a position to disgrace you. Wreck you. You see it, don't you?"

She couldn't look at him. "I see," she said, dully. "You mean it's holding onto you . . . that half-world?"

"It's not as easy as I'd expected to break free. There's a couple of people . . . well, I won't go into it. They're insecure, hysterical people to begin with. They look on me as a deserter. You've heard the saying that nothing's deadlier than a woman scorned. In their cases, they're worse than women. Very vengeful."

"Just so long as you *are* a deserter. Tom, tell me the truth. Since me, you haven't ever been tempted to slip back. . . ?

His mouth got tight and angry, and his eyes were distressed. She took his suddenly clenched fist in her hands, stroked it.

"Forgive me. I don't want an answer. I trust you. I know you. Even if you ever were tempted I'd understand you didn't want to be, that you *do* love me, Tom."

"I'll take care of everything . . . get free. Put a stop to the blackmail. I can. I'm sure . . . almost sure. But frankly, I'm broke, Mimi. I'll have to teach the summer session."

It was decided. She would keep her job. At least for a few more months. She didn't mind. A "triffle," she thought, remembering Mr. Ceccini with a wistful smile. Tom was going to buy her a new piano as a wedding gift. They were going to start shopping for one tomorrow morning, in fact. As she went into her favorite cafeteria for breakfast Friday morning she was thinking about that and about the luscious new meaning of her paycheck two hours from now and about the beginning of the new weekend with Tom that afternoon.

Mimi set down her tray, put her folded newspaper and purse on the chair, moved over to the rack and hung her coat and returned swingily, a pert smile on her face. A placidly munching stranger caught the wave of her smile, and grinned and his eyes blinked with unexpected pleasure. The sun from outside glowed on her bright hair and lovely face and appetite made her eyes shine with childish greediness. Her mouth was watering by the time she'd arranged her toast, egg, juice and coffee. She seated herself, looking daintily charming in a crisp white pleat-front blouse.

She didn't eat a bite.

Her newspaper lying folded on the slope of her purse on the next chair began to rise up, unfolding. It opened out full length with a light flapping sound revealing again the unpleasant front page. Mimi looked with distaste at the violent, sneering face of a young tough covering almost the whole page. A thick black double headline above read:

121

MURDER AND SUICIDE
IN LOCAL "LOVE NEST"

Under "Nest" it said Story on Page Five. She started to refold the paper and secure it under her purse, when she saw the name below the picture.

Tom Wilks. Tom Wilks? She looked at the picture with mingled distaste and resentment that this ugly hoodlum had the same name as Tom. Then something like a clock spring embedded under the diaphragm in her upper abdomen began to wind, tightening a little. She drew her feet and knees together, turned on her chair and held the paper in front of her. The face was young, half Tom's age, and caught in a vivid expression of fierce defiance or aggression. She looked at the forehead's breadth, the general upside-down-triangle of the face's basic structure and groped out on the table feeling for her glass of ice water which she'd forgot to get. She wet her lips with her tongue.

She turned back to page five, overshot, found page eleven. She coughed and began to squirm. It could or couldn't be of Tom long ago, a picture clipped out of an action shot of a whole gang and blown up. . . . She found page five and there was pictured a bed and a body and black bloody splotches, and another body on a chair. Clothed bodies, ghastly with death. There was another picture: a knife, "the murder-suicide" weapon. The face of the man in the chair was Tom Wilks.

The story was written with crude sneers. The tragedy had taken place in an unnamed hotel where shouts and sounds of struggle had been heard around midnight. Hotel detectives and police breaking in at 1 a.m. had found the bodies. The hotel room was referred to as a love nest; the other man had been convicted as a homosexual; Tom's juvenile gang past and teaching present were linked with "sordid" associations with known homosexuals, dismissal from public schools on complaints of a molested student, etc., etc.

She read and re-read the story and wanted to get up and go somewhere and do something. She couldn't. The blood seemed to have drawn out of her extremities; her feet and legs were numb, her hands cold, her head faint.

122

She just sat taking long, slow breaths. The wall and the cashier and the in-and-out lines of customers swirled and lost their actuality and became blurs of sight and garbled sound . . . in the next minute everything everybody was saying and doing was distinct but totally incomprehensible. She got a finger hooked into her coffeecup handle, lifted and spilled half a saucerful and put it down.

"Well, it's like you know it's where if two times one point I where we went forward," she mumbled.

She scratched her nose and smiled. Almost time for work. She must buy a paper somewhere. She got her coat and purse and paid her check. Outside, she went the wrong direction. She stopped and bought all the papers. She went in another cafeteria and read. The thing she found out was that the Dalles Funeral Home on Second Avenue would know.

They knew. She couldn't see him before that night, but they knew. Yes. She phoned Mrs. Cobb, the Welfare woman who had been so sweet and sympathetic during her pregnancy and after Barbie was born. Mrs. Cobb was always glad to talk to her and see her.

Mrs. Cobb phoned the police and found out for sure. Yes. Then she came to the funeral home that night and sat with Mimi. Members of Tom's family she'd never seen were there. They wondered about her and watched her whenever she stood beside the open casket. Once she started to reach in and touch his beautiful face and they took her away.

During the funeral service she just stared hollowly and listened to the talk and became nauseated by the flower odor. When the organ played the Chopin prelude that he and she had listened to over and over and over Mimi broke down and began to sob inconsolably and Mrs. Cobb had to take her out.

She didn't go to the cemetery but to Mrs. Cobb's apartment. Mrs. Cobb watched over her like she thought she'd kill herself. Mimi kept going over it and over it and trying to figure out what really had happened. Surely, surely it had been one of the blackmailers and he'd been trying to hold onto Tom and bleed him to death the rest of his life and Tom had stopped him. Or.

Or Tom had been tempted to slip back into the other

life. The craving had come over him like he said, like an insanity. After he'd slipped and realized what he had done he'd gone mad with shame and killed his tempter and himself. If, two months ago he had slipped he would not have been as tortured as that. Only since she had brought him the gift of her love, she thought bitterly, the beautiful gift of her precious love to disrupt the pattern he had learned to live with had he found his lapses unbearable. Mimi began to cheer up and smile and talk about things in a balanced way. Mrs. Cobb decided it was safe to let her go home.

Mimi went back to her apartment. The other girls wouldn't be home from work for a couple of hours. She wrote a note and thumb-tacked it to the door. Then she went into the bathroom, drew a tub and got in. She rested her head on the rack pillow and lay there feeling physically comfortable for awhile, thinking wryly how she had probably demonstrated an old saying about the road to hell being paved with good intentions.

She took the razor blade from the edge of the tub, rinsed it and studied her wrists. Everything she'd had . . . love, best intentions . . . she'd thrown into the fight. In the nick of time she had saved Tom Wilks from a life of shame. She smiled. So he was dead.

First she cut her left wrist. Then she cut her right wrist. She watched the blood coming out for a little while and began to cry softly. She shut her eyes and just relaxed and let herself drift away, thinking "Goodbye . . . anybody . . . goodbye. . . ." She sighed deeply and slept.

She didn't welcome the efforts of her roommates. She was not grateful to the ambulance surgeon. She did not give a damn that he decided to list it as an accident so she wouldn't be held in the psychiatric ward. She didn't give a damn, period. When Randy Partch came around with flowers and thought she'd done it because of him and might cause him to lose his job she felt like groaning.

"Don't worry, little girl. No one will know of this . . . I've sworn your roomies to secrecy. . . . We'll get married as soon as you're up and strong enough. . . . You haven't mentioned anything to anyone at the office, have you?"

"No."

"You're sure you're pregnant?"

"Sure I'm *not*."

"Well, why. . . .?"

"Forget it."

"Everybody's going to *think* you were. I'll marry you, anyway! I promise."

"Thanks," she said bitterly. When he was gone she had an uncontrollable fit of laughter.

✤ FOURTEEN ✤

THE WEDDING ANNOUNCEMENT created a stir among the girls at the office. Those who'd been casual became friendly; the friendlier ones became romantically involved, took up collections and planned a shower and a restaurant party.

The atmosphere surrounding the wedding involved her in all the externals so that she hardly noticed the central fact that it was a bad and false marriage. She confided in Mrs. Cobb.

"The wedding day keeps getting closer. And though I know I don't love him and know I'm being false, I'll probably just not have the energy to stop before I'm married. Sometimes I think I should just disappear. What do you think, Mrs. Cobb?"

"Well, Mimi, look at your mother. Diane is a *marv*'lous woman," she allowed herself a smile, a moment's secret admiration of Diane, "but *look* at her. I don't want you floundering that way, off-balance, off-base, constantly harried. You'll thrive in a proper environment. Go on and marry him. It's what you need. And Mimi," she added, rather grimly, "what you need you take!"

Unexpectedly Randy's male colleagues warmed to him. Just after offering marriage Randy had acted like a philanthropist with a toothache when alone with her. But one evening he crowed:

"The gang didn't think I had it in me. They think you're great."

"Among the girls," Mimi said politely, "I've taken a step up in status."

"It's a kick making 'em green with envy, right?" He gargled a short laugh, then said importantly: "Jameson in-

126

vited me to lunch." Jameson, a V.P., was head of Randy's division.

"I'm glad to hear it," she said with insufficient enthusiasm.

" 'I'm glad to hear it,' " he mimicked. *"Jameson,* I said, invited *me* to lunch."

"If you feel like that, I'd just as soon call it off."

"Are you crazy? Call it off when everybody's expecting it? You can't just call a thing off that's all planned, arrangements made. You look here. . . ."

"Don't point your finger at me!"

"I guess you're still upset from that crazy thing you did. You'll be O.K. We don't want to upset the applecart now when everything's going big."

"I'd better explain," Mimi decided. "I was in love with a man who wasn't free to marry me. I had given up and that's why I went to your apartment that night. I expected it to lead to marriage. Security. Meantime, the other man was suddenly free. He loved me too. By now I'd have been *his* wife. He was killed in an accident. That's why I did that crazy thing, as you call it. I don't want to do a crazier thing. I don't love you."

While she talked Randy sat at the end of the sofa, half turned toward her, watching her face closely. When she was finished he looked down at his hands, lying slack. His mouth drooped. She felt a pang of sympathy and reached over and patted his hand.

"I didn't mean to hurt you. But you had to know."

"Yes, I had to know." He nodded dejectedly. He stood up, shaking his head, and walked to the window. "I always have to know." He came back, shrugged, and picked up his hat. "I'm glad at this moment . . . maybe for the first time in my life . . . that I am what I am. If I were really a human being, capable of experiencing that great and mysterious thing called love, I might go out and do a crazy thing too. There are times when emotional cripplement is an advantage. I'll withstand this better than a human being would."

The defeat in his shoulders as he turned toward the door made her go to him. She put her arm around his shoulder and tried to peer into his face. He turned away.

"Randy, don't go this way. Don't say you're not a human being. I didn't mean to give you that feeling."

He slipped an arm around her waist, gave her a companionable hug and a forced smile.

"Of course I knew I wasn't first choice, Mimi. I knew I was second, third . . . tenth. I didn't worry. I'm used to the leavings. I'd have been glad to get them. . . . I still would be, Mimi!"

Taking his hands Mimi drew him back to the couch, her eyes gravely sympathetic. Randy sat down tiredly.

"I never tell anybody this, Mimi, I'm too proud, so please don't let it go any farther. I don't know who my parents were," he said. "Maybe I was a bastard, maybe turned over by impoverished parents. No matter. My first memories are of the Home . . . a big dorm . . . a gray life. . . . Couples would come on Sunday and look us over while we were cleaned up and at our best. . . . You never knew when lightning would strike and you'd be taken and loved . . . well, let's not get mawkish.

"Anyway I was always among the unchosen. Later I boarded around at various homes, became no real part of any of them. I fought to educate myself, earn my B.S. I got into Drayton-Blieling and I've made good in a moderate way . . . but it was always as though, in the eyes of the bosses, I was barely up to my job. I felt my promotions were always on a basis of least-worst."

"Now, Randy, you know in a hard-headed business organization it couldn't have been so. You feel undervalued because of your childhood. . . . I think it's so sad, that kind of childhood, Randy. I mean it, and I'm sorry. If only I'd known all these things about you and had learned to see and understand you *before*. But I can at least help you see that your feelings about not being appreciated in your job are wrong."

"I can tell you a scientific term for it, as far as that goes. It's neurotic. I'm applying the attitudes of one situation to another irrelevant situation. I know about that. Mimi, it doesn't help. The unchangeable fact is that I am personally unlovable; which is justice, because I am unloving. I can't feel love with any certainty. There's a psychological theory about *that,* too.

"Love, it says, is a learned response. If it isn't learned early it comes hard. You don't really know what it is or how to give it. I instinctively groped toward a quality in you, warmth, a female knowledge, a something. And I

128

was correct. Everybody likes you. In a sense, my connection with you has warmed away the fog that surrounded me and made me invisible. Because of you, people now see me as at least potentially a human person.

"I'm suddenly estimated good enough to be noticed by the big boss himself. He's going to buy me a meal. A small, silly thing to become excited about, I suppose, but . . . well, it's not merely its significance to my future, Jameson's taking me to lunch. It's the fact that he will be making a gesture of personal acceptance. . . . Oh, well . . . if the fog settles around me again, I can exist as before."

"Randy, you're making me ashamed."

"No, Mimi, I'm not reproaching you. You see, I'd hoped like this . . . that we'd learn together to care for each other . . . that if I was good to you and earned your approval you would give me meanings. Teach me the profound things that a woman knows. But of course there are many women and with my steady job I'll attract something . . . not a you, Mimi, but . . ." He slumped for a silent moment. "Please marry me. Mimi. With you I'll rise. I'll earn more. Not for the sake of the money or position, not really . . . though these things in the past have had to substitute for every other lack. Mimi, we could give each other security, Mimi . . . financial and emotional. . . . *Please* don't back out."

"All right, Randy."

As he was leaving he promised, "I'll tell you about the lunch with Jameson."

Mr. Jameson had been friendly and encouraging; he'd congratulated him on the step he was taking and assured him that the company was watching his progress with satisfaction. Randy spent two hours interpreting the possible meanings involved. He allowed a trifle grudgingly that Mimi might be an asset to his career.

So . . . though she didn't love him . . . not yet . . . and sometimes didn't even like him . . . they were married.

Mimi had been afraid of the wake of the wedding activities when inexorably she'd be alone with and firmly attached to his life. But the honeymoon was full of outside distractions, travel, restaurants, hotels, new settings, pleasant outside interests. She stayed focussed on and got through the intimacies tolerably because in his feverish states Randy barely noticed her uninvolvement.

Focussing outward was the secret of the marriage itself. There was the nice six room two-story leased house, the brand new furniture, concern with the thousand problems of materials and equipment. They had some sort of social activity two or three times a week. Guests, visits, cards provided distractions. Other times there was blessed television to divert their attentions from each other during uncomfortable alone-together periods. And there were all kinds of routine matters to go into, and sometimes, too, he worked. Days she had her house and reading. She joined women's card groups, a music club; she bought records. She made several friendships and had in Mrs. Cobb a confidante who always, whatever she did, assured her she was right.

In a year she conscientiously achieved something for them both, she was sure. She had studied and become proficient at entertaining his business associates and their wives. He was pleased with himself and evidently things went well at work. Because she understood and felt a responsibility and sympathy for him she suppressed her dislike of his fawning with superiors and arrogance with subordinates.

She tried to broach the subject but he got nasty with her. She tried not to take such things personally, knowing it was a defense mechanism, to cover deep pains and that eventually he wouldn't need to be as he was. Her gestures and words of affection were never spontaneous, always calculated, something she gave because it was needed.

She tried, with little success, to feel that because . . . like Tom, in a way . . . Randy was a flawed creature, she must be endlessly sympathetic. He himself had few spontaneous gestures and almost no tenderness, but, maybe, he tried. Though she didn't notice any transformation, he spoke of having come to know true love.

One night, after they'd entertained his section chief, Randy got boastfully drunk.

"Not only have I got true love, dear sharp little bedmate and social-business partner, but also as a result of my sock-away program since my first D-B paycheck I've

130

got something of value. $21,802.74. Don't blab it around or try to find out *where* I've got it invested."

"I don't like your way of putting things," she said exasperatedly.

"Excuse my being an ox in the artistic presence of such a dainty soul. The way you throw that arty crap around the dinner table in front of guests!"

"Randy, I know you don't *want* to be this way so I'm not going to take offense."

"Instead of take offense, take off your pense, cute ass!"

She looked at him disgustedly.

"Don't give me that!" he flashed. "If I got to take it away from you I will."

With an icy calm that surprised him Mimi said: "I advise you, never, as long as you live, to try anything like that. I advise you!"

"Ah, to hell with it," he said and had another drink.

There was a sexual advantage to wifehood; no need to endure a buildup. Mimi was ready and waiting for his thrice weekly revels. Before and after her periods he added a session, as if he had a balance sheet somewhere that must total twelve or thirteen a month.

There was a Sunday morning pattern. Breakfast was late and leisurely. They both read the papers at the table. When she got up to clear the table his hand would reach out and pat her bottom. The minute he did it Mimi would turn and walk out of the kitchen unzipping her dress, shorts, slacks or whatever she was wearing and she would be on the bed when he came.

Her instant sex-machine response had a double advantage. It was speedy and it irritated him. He knew she didn't enjoy sex, but every once in awhile when he'd had a particularly good time he got coy and wanted her to tell him the truth about her own feelings.

He got the truth and learned to quit asking. He spread it around that she was frigid . . . thinking it might steer men off. What it did was incite them to make passes, positive that the frigidity couldn't be her fault. She brushed off the passes and might have stayed sexless if Jock Standish hadn't reappeared when she'd been married just over two years.

Since leaving Drayton-Blieler he'd been in three different jobs. In one he put through a plan opening up an un-tapped market for a competitor of D-B. . . . an idea re-fused by D-B.

On another job on the West Coast he'd organized a purchasing and warehousing system involving several hun-dred small manufacturers. His work there had been written up as a feature in an important trade publication.

At a lodge dinner dance Jock talked about it lengthily. The half-dozen other men, including Randy, were all from D-B and listened fascinatedly to the details. Jock's interest ran out. He smiled over at Mimi.

"How about a dance, Mimi?" She nodded, smiling.

"O.K., Randy?"

"Go on."

She wore a wispy blue chiffon halter dress, her hair in a long straight bob swinging inches above her bare shoul-ders. Jock wore a white tuxedo and his square face was bronzed handsomely. The tips of his short dark brown hair were golden. He took her in his arms and they moved, turning easily.

"Did you use bleach or sunlight on the tips of your hair to get the halo effect?"

"Produced by myriad fairies with beads of sunlight on tiny wands," he said sourly, and gave her a grotesque, stretched smile. "They also whitewashed my teeth. With the tan very seductive, what?"

"Yes."

"You know your hair looks like pouring honey? Do you spend more time these days prettifying yourself? Being narcissistic, you should."

"Admiring myself, you mean? No." Her reply was crisp.

"What do you do with the libido, then? It's not fixed on him."

"It's fixed on many things. My house. Books. Music. Friends. Including you."

She became aware of how totally Jock was absorbed with her. Mimi knew that what she said was a matter of indifference, except that the high, clear feminine sound of her voice and the motion of her lips added to the fascina-tion she held for him.

The orchestra was playing a lovely arrangement of *Wonderful One,* a cello giving the strings body. Jock began to sing quietly in a smooth baritone. "My wonderful one. . . ." He looked at her steadily as he sang. Their bodies moved effortlessly together flowing with the melodic rhythm. His singing was a clear, direct statement to her and for her alone. The whole mood was so beautiful that her eyes brimmed.

At the end of the lyrics his arm pressed her a little more closely and he nodded slowly as if saying "Yes, that's true, I do feel that way . . . you are my wonderful one . . . and you and I, Mimi, know each other's hearts, there is a special bond and understanding . . . we belong together. . . ."

"Oh, Jock, it's so good to have you back."

"I've missed you, Mimi. We've waited a long time for each other, sweetheart."

"I want you so much. So much!" She bit her lip, her eyes distressed. "Can it be soon? It must be! Even tonight. . . . Yes," she said tensely. The music stopped. They returned to the table.

Five hours later at seven past two, Mimi lay in the dark listening remotely to Randy's song, a drunken snore while Jock Standish's image floated in and out of her consciousness. She sat up on her bed and, catching the hem òf her baby-doll nightgown, lifted it, unveiling her body, the sensation of the material on her skin like whispering lips. She extended her arms full length overhead, elongating her bare body, narrowing the curve of her waist and raising her conical breasts high.

Imagining that Jock observed every action with tenderly loving eyes, Mimi swayed to one side, making herself consciously pleasing, her body momentarily shaping an *houri's* attitude of supple, yielding grace.

She released the nightgown and let it fall floatily. Turning, she lowered her feet daintily, pointing the toes and gliding them into satin mules, then stood up. She left the room soundlessly, her hands angling up femininely from the wrists and feeling out for balance at her sides.

She had already bathed and creamed her body and retouched her dark red toenail polish. Now in the bathroom she put on her prettiest, scented underthings, feeling that each detail of tiny bow, ribbon, lace, and feminine colors would add a morsel of delight to Jock's pleasure.

Then, like plain brownpaper package wrapping, she put

133

on a casual overlayer: ordinary skirt, blouse, ankle socks and mocs. She covered her hair with a print scarf, watching the articulations of her curving quick fingers, the pink lacquer flashings of her long oval fingernails. At the last moment she used more perfume, a light, fresh scent, touching the tips of her bra, her throat, wrists and palms. She drew a long breath and went downstairs. Randy's snore sounded through the whole house.

She took a sweater from the closet, hung it around her shoulders and stood looking out the door window at the pleasant, broad residential street, asleep and calm at this hour. She held a forefinger to the hollow of her throat feeling the pulse, now calm and measured, then rushing with each distant sound of a car's acceleration. She curved her wrist up, peered at her luminous dial watch. Two twenty-five. Five more minutes. A minute later her heart leaped at sight of a low black sportster, decelerating quietly, stopping. Mimi hurried out to Jock.

The car nosed into a parking space of a large motel. They went up a stairs and along a railed walk. She stood against him while he unlocked the door. Inside the blinds were shut and shaded light glowed on neat chairs, small tables, two beds . . . one turned down. He held his hands out and moved to her as she was moving to him, her face tilting back, her eyes closing. She caught her breath just before his lips brushed hers.

For a split second she had a dreadful stabbingly violent headache, then the sensation and almost her whole consciousness washed away as though on a torrent. His mouth, hot and mobile, kissed her lips urgently. She began to shiver. Her knees actually shook and her hands were trembling so badly that she seized him as much to control herself as to embrace him.

While he was kissing her he felt her body, his slow, possessive touch moved and paused, his warm broad hands fitting to the contours of her shoulders, her sides, the small of her back, the flare and round of her hips. Her buttocks clenched when he touched her there and she arched forward against him.

He kissed her two or three times, standing, and then the excess of sensation seemed to flood them both at once and

134

they moved away from each other. She drew a long breath and dropped to a seated position on the bed, drew her feet out of her mocs, her gaze following him, then silently pulling him to her. He came and sat by her and took off her head scarf. She'd arranged her hair in undulating lines that rose over her ear and dropped away, gently curving to her nape.

She gestured, tracing the line for him to see and he kissed her fingers, her ear, her throat. She could feel a slow throbbing in her lips, and they felt hot and pleasantly swollen. She lay on her back, unbuttoning her blouse, and put her feet on the bed, her knees lifted, while Jock walked away to take off his clothes.

Mimi removed her blouse and skirt and lay with one hand languidly on her blue net bra, the other on her high cut lace-edged panties. She pulled a long breath and arched upward, stroking her belly with half-conscious voluptuousness, pushing the top of her panties a little below her navel. She saw him coming, his angular male, deep-chested body bronzed and strong. He wore only a brief garment like a pure white arrow at the base of his flat stomach.

He came on the bed and lay kissing her mouth while his hands strokingly, unhurriedly removed her panties, then her bra. He kept drawing away, prolonging everything, sometimes kissing her body and her breasts, at other times her mouth, while his hands caressed her lingeringly. She felt her own desirability in the touch of his hands, his eyes, and in his occasional word of tenderness.

Then she did not know any more how she looked or how she might be pleasing him; her consciousness of herself was gone and she moved in a remote, almost bodiless atmosphere of pure sensation, every inch of her skin tingled. Waves of warmth and small delicious spasms of pleasure caught at her breasts and belly and intimate inner flesh.

Before he even covered her she was suddenly swept to a rushing climax. She stared up at him with tense, anxious eyes, knowing he knew she had reached fulfillment. Yet there was scarcely any diminishing of her desire and when he moved above her she yielded herself to him. When he was totally merged with her her senses flared. She felt a sudden acute awareness in every fiber of her body and coiled her limbs around him trying to fuse every part of herself with his body.

The feeling of being carried that Jock had always given her now reached a heightened intensity. She became part of a blissful wavelike movement as supple as the sea and as strong. When his tempo quickened it had the elemental excitement of approaching storm. She thrilled to the powerful rise of his tension and felt strong with his strength, lifted as by a defiance mighty enough to shatter the power of gravity itself, thrusting them to unknown heights, and a wild, unbearably sweet, shuddering ecstasy. It was followed by a long, lazily soaring descent, a comfortably throbbing diminuendo and sleep, dreamless, desireless, sleep.

She woke fresh within twenty minutes, with a glorious sense of having expressed all her passion to completion. Jock lay curled on his side, his leg across her body, his arm across her chest, his hand in sleep curved around her shoulder. She lay enjoying the mild discomfort and feel of loving captivity. She roused him seductively. He moved in his sleep and was in the process of possessing her again before he was fully awake. . . . His startled pleasure at finding himself not in a dream was so delightful that Mimi made a purring sound in her throat. And while he was loving her he laughed with her.

"Sweetheart," he said, "Did you ever have so damned much fun in your whole life?"

"Never. Let's never stop. Oooooh!! LOVER!"

They slept and woke again at daylight. She got up and dressed hurriedly, a little alarmed. Jock drove her to within a block of home. She went in as if she'd been for an early walk. Randy was up with a sick hangover and too grateful for aspirins, cold tomato juice and soothing ministrations to ask questions.

Jock was due to leave town in a week and they tried to get their fill, arranging trysts to make love at least once a day. He left on schedule. Mimi was grateful for the jewel week and resolved not to spoil it with the after pains of loneliness, and fell back into vigorous routine. Afterwards Jock was in and out of town for long or short periods three or four times a year and gradually, in an emotional sense, they got married.

136

No other man but Tom Wilks had ever known so much about her. Mimi gave him her whole past, in bits and pieces. Jock pried it out of her, wanting to possess her as totally as she wanted him to, so that he could carry her around wherever he was. Yet there was no future for them. They had each other's pasts, and the best of immediate moments, but they didn't plan ahead for themselves.

Jock didn't even tell her about any of his projects or job possibilities until they were actualities. Though when . . . as he very often was . . . he was "between jobs" he told her about the last one he'd had. He scorned as sentimental her feeling that she must recompense Randy for childhood unhappiness, and suggested she really hung on for her own security . . . or at least the *sense* of security.

"That's all you've really got there, the *sense* of security. You yourself create it. He's unreliable, Mimi. Far more so than *I* am . . ." When she couldn't avoid a slightly bitter laugh, he said angrily, "Let's get over this idea that because I move by my own initiative from top job to top job that I'm worse off than if I droned away in one particular prison. If you had any guts you'd take a chance on me . . . slack periods and all!"

"All right. When? I'll marry you! Like that!"

She snapped her fingers.

"Leave him tomorrow. We'll get married."

"Good. Now let's have some fun now. Let's go to bed."

"Don't get aggressive, Mimi!"

"Let's face it, Jock. The idea of being tied down to me stops you cold. The minute I'm ready to marry you things get grim between us. I suddenly become as alluring to you as dishwater. Forget it. So let's go on the way we are. This way you do love me. And that's what makes my life, Jock. It's everything to me. Love me, darling."

✣ FIFTEEN ✣

SHE WAS TRUE to her "two husbands" until she was twenty-five and Randy's income and position had brought him up above the $12,500 income line that separated him from "lower-middle" management. They contracted for a new ranch house on an acre of landscaped ground in a fairly exclusive suburb with winding streets, in the radius of Dartmoor Country Club.

Mr. Jameson himself and equal income men from other companies belonged there, as well as scores of important D-B middle and upper executives and when Randy was accepted he announced the great word with an excitement such as she only saw when he was in heat . . . even the pink splotches came out on his face. He was a little paunchy and his face was fuller with beginning jowls, so that his close-set features seemed even more pinched into the middle of his face. He stated with his growing air of superior knowledge that he'd become more handsome.

They were almost at the lowest rung of the income ladder in that area, rubbing fenders with Jags, Rollses, Bentleys, Mercedez-Benzes. The club dues were high, the fees for everything expensive, the special events requiring much more in the way of clothes, especially for her if Randy Partch's property was going to shine out the way he wanted. Their yard and grill, patio and furniture for outside entertaining, became items of expense and the liquor bills went up. Mimi fell into the company of women who visited the more elegant salons and shops.

She developed a certain hauteur. Around her mouth was a touch of disdain, partly a conscious imitation of Tom. Her eyes were level and she had a way of looking at a man showing interest in her body as if she were undressing him, too, and finding him wanting. It challenged a lot of them and if they wanted her desperately she slept with them.

She played cards in day-long sessions at the club or at other wives' homes or her own. She spent more and more time in beauty salons and in the pampering, perfuming, lotioning and the clothing of her body. She dressed with the care of an actress for even the most informal occasion. At dances, at the club pool on "Bikini Beach," costume parties, she displayed herself.

Living was expensive. Randy began to watch her primping at her dressing table, becoming more beautiful, wearing expensive clothes he had to provide and hated to pay for and he'd mutter:

"You're breaking me."

"Let's drop down to a social level we can afford, then."

He wanted to increase the number of sex sessions.

"They're going to decrease," she told him.

Once he ordered her like a drill sergeant to go to bed with him. Very calmly she went to the kitchen, got a knife. She lay on the bed with the knife.

"All right, Randy," she said with a faint smile. "Come on," she coaxed. "I wish you would!"

Jock had more or less settled down in the general area, maintaining a shack by the sea thirty miles away. It was elegant and modern with a rocky view and a half mile of private beach. He earned very high fees which Randy knew all too well, and it was a grim point of hostility, and Jock's "in between" periods were sources of Randy's greatest pleasure. He hopefully predicted that the boy genius had at last come to the end of his "fluke flashes of inspiration" and would never have another.

Mimi had not seen Jock in two months when she visited him at the shack. They were lying in swim suits on the deck listening to the sea and getting a tan when Jock said:

"It's the sense of security you get from him, you create it all. Day by day, Mimi, you are falsifying life more and more. Consequently your perceptions are dulling, restricting, shutting out truth and hopes of a healthy future. You are, in fact, regressing."

"That's a good example of what you explained 'projection' was. You feel yourself slipping backward, so you accuse me."

139

He sat up, got up and went inside. He came back in sweater and pants and tossed her shoes and clothes beside her. "We'll go for a walk. You're right. Projection. You counter-projected, though. We're both slipping back. I can see us reaching middle age as mental infants. . . . Come on, doll, I'm troubled. Let's walk and throw stones at the damned ocean."

That's just what they did. He was in a muttering mood and preferred silence. She wasn't prepared for what he blurted.

"What would you think of a man who asked his widowed mother and unmarried sister for seven percent interest on a signed note? People in trouble, needing two thousand badly? These women run a small grocery in the city. Had it for years. When this man was going to college they mortgaged the place and had a rotten time paying off.

"As a kid his older sisters, his father and mother catered to him and spoiled him. They said he was too bright to waste time helping in the store. They put him through college. He got a job and turned his back on them. He denies their existence if possible.

"A week ago they forced their way back into his life. The sister and mother needed money for modernized equipment. Otherwise the big stores would finally squeeze them out of existence. He had never paid back a dime on his education. He denied he owed them anything; asked to see any note he'd ever signed, then wanted *them* to sign a note before he'd kick through. Rotten!"

"Did they get the money from him?"

"Finally. He didn't dare let it become known generally on his job. I got it from Jake Bover down at D-B.

"Someone at Drayton-Blieling? Who?"

"The pitiful orphan you married."

"I don't believe it . . . I mean, Jock, I can't believe it. It's incredible. You sure they're his real family?"

"Absolutely. You want to go to that grocery store?"

"Yes!"

It proved to be shockingly true! She didn't know how she could ever look at Randy again. He came home that night blustering because she hadn't come to the station to pick him up. She was packing her clothes.

She turned and with fists on hips said: "Shut up! The

only truth you told me, Partch, was that you're a bastard! I was talking today with your sister and mother."

For once he didn't have a word to say. He walked out of the house.

Mimi moved to a hotel. He came and begged her to return, to consider herself separated, but to live with him temporarily. On another visit he brought a detective's report of her visits to Jock and to two other men, and assured her he'd fight a divorce and fight dirty. Nonetheless she didn't return.

A week later she was at Jock's shack. He kept talking about Randy till she called a halt:

"I didn't come here to hear about him. But to be loved."

She went over to the bunk and began to undress.

"I'm jobless," he told her bluntly. "Maybe I'll never have another idea. It looks now as though I *will* have to take a plodding, hateful prisonlike job. . . ."

"To take care of me?"

"What else? I'm in analysis. Thirty-five dollars an hour five days a week. I can't keep up that kind of expense very long on my reserve if we have to . . . oh, hell, Mimi, this isn't what I mean. I'm scared. What happened to your friend Tom Wilks . . . it happened to me. A month ago. I'm a dead man, sexually. It happened three or four times in the past, but cured spontaneously after a few days. This one's severe. I'm up against some hidden monster. I don't know how long . . . at thirty-five dollars a day . . . it'll take to dig it out. Maybe YEARS." He shook his head violently. "I've been covering something up too long . . . now it's so deep, so cunning and deadly. . . ."

She went to him and petted his face, looking deeply into his eyes. She could almost always lift his depressions. "You'll get over it," she said. "Tom did. And his had lasted for *years.*"

She half-smiled, feeling the grisly joke about it, but she sobered fast. It was no joke with him. He was facing the sun and the harsh light revealed stress lines like knife cuts at the corners of his mouth. His naked anxiety surfaced to his eyes, dipped out of sight again, but just the glimpse was frightening.

"Was there anything special about that occasion when

141

he found he could love you, Mimi? What fixed him? Just a growing awareness of how much he loved you, I suppose." He turned and walked away dispiritedly. "My awareness is complete."

She went to the bunk without further words, undressed completely, a quick, panicky excitement in her at the exultant realization that she, she alone, knew the magic. She would bring his aggression into play alongside his sex; lash him till he raged and hated and wanted to smash out. The drive of it, teamed with his love would restore his manliness, no doubt at all.

Nonetheless, she tried first to seduce him. She brought into play everything she knew that roused him. He kept moving away from her, in and out of every room. He sat. He stood. Occasionally he stretched out, trying to respond. His kisses were mechanical.

She finally took a long breath and looked at him as at a stranger and enemy and began to lash him with verbal scorn till he winced and flinched and grew pale. Finally he ran from her. He came back and gathered her clothes in a ball, hurling them at her as if he wished they were made of steel. He went out and downstairs and out toward the beach.

"Wait," she cried. "Jock . . . come back up. . . ." She ran naked to the top of the steps, and looked down at him, her eyes frantic. "That was it! The thing that brought Tom back. I got him furious. . . . I didn't ever tell you he ever felt anything but love for me. But I roused his *hate*, too. That's what I was doing for *you*, darling . . . don't misunderstand."

"Don't you know that an assault like that on a man in my condition is dangerous? Deadly? I'll tell you the truth, Mimi, it almost killed you! For a moment I didn't know you. *I didn't know you.* I just saw a deadly enemy that I had to destroy. I'm a complex man, Mimi. You can't blast away problems like mine with that kind of kid stuff. We're going to have to break it off, Mimi. Pull stunts like that and you'll blow us both to hell. We'll stay in touch, Mimi, but we'll shallow out. I can't absorb intensities like that at this time."

Thereafter they stayed in touch and out of touch. They saw each other and though they yearned for each other they were horribly apart. Mimi returned to Randy's house

142

and began to play around in earnest, having affairs with several men.

She marked time in her part of Randy's house and it might have gone on that way till the dreary end of time. But one night while she was preparing to dress for a formal dinner they were attending Randy, in slippers and robe, came into her bedroom without knocking. Fresh from a bath Mimi was sitting naked at her dresser, applying lotion to her shoulders and breasts.

"Get out," she said, watching him narrowly in the mirror as he came across the room behind her. She lifted the thick purple towel from her legs, lay it across her pale breasts. He stopped, stood at her back.

"We're going to bed," he said grittily, looking down at her.

"We're not going to bed," Mimi said evenly.

He unlooped his robe belt, peeled off the robe. He was naked. He inched forward, touched her smooth bare back. Mimi recoiled.

"Get away from me. Don't you dare touch me."

"You luscious bitch!" He reached over, caught the towel and threw it on the floor. His hands came down over her shoulders, his fingers embedded in the softness of her breasts. He pushed his body against her back. She twisted to one side, leaped up and ran. He caught one arm and yanked her back to him. His right hand held her wrist and forced her arm painfully up between her shoulder blades. His other hand coiled around her body, gliding over the soft smoothness of her lower belly. With a swift double motion Mimi bumped backward then pitched forward. He wrenched her arm up her back violently; the pain was so raw and sharp that she cried out.

"Damn you, let me GO! I warn you, Randy! Let go of me."

For answer he yanked her arm again, and maintaining the pressure and pain he forced her to walk on tiptoe to the bed. He was panting and at the same time half-laughing.

At the edge of the bed he pushed her forward, fell on top of her and held her face down while he used her vilely. She lay biting the covers, tears of rage and outrage welling in her eyes. When he left she cursed him in a low voice.

143

"I'll get you," she called after him. "I'll get you for this!"

She hated him but couldn't decide what to do to him. Another night she woke to find he'd sneaked in and tied her wrists and ankles to the bedposts. He raped her. A week later Mimi made a gesture of reconciliation as preparation for gaining his trust, so that she could destroy him.

A few days later he was upset by a small episode. They dined at the club. Mr. Jameson entered the dining room, walked past him with the curtest of acknowledgments. The atmosphere scared Randy.

He fretted aloud till finally Mimi said: "He's guilty. He wants me."

"How come he can't get you?"

"He's worth something; why should I give it away? I've got an idea."

"What?"

"Later."

Mr. Jameson was in his fifties, a taut, nervous man with thinning gray hair and, seasonally, a tan, since he golfed a lot. In general, he maintained a wall of impeccable manners around himself. He had been a widower for three years and he'd only recently begun to escort a few older women now and then. In Mimi's set he was a subject of endless discussion. In the same breath the young wives praised his devotion to his late wife and criticized his failure to re-marry or at least take a mistress.

His attitude to Mimi was shy, courteous appreciation; but occasionally, after drinks at a dance, for instance, his interest was bolder. Once he'd been in a deck chair when she walked along the Club pool with a flower in the hip strings of her bikini. She'd gone on to lie on "Bikini Beach," a section behind circusy striped canvas at one end of the pool area. There the women lay nearly nude, absorbing sunlight on upturned hips, backs or fronts of their bodies.

There was a second floor porch on the clubhouse overlooking "Bikini Beach" and men often observed the scene from there. From that angle the top of the canvas cut off the women's heads or feet, depending on which way they were turned, so that they seemed like so much pampered flesh, warming and waiting . . . the men enjoyed the view.

144

The day Mimi passed Mr. Jameson with the flower on her hip he made a rare visit to the observation deck. Mimi had been lying on her back, her pillowed head facing him. Another girl who had become something of a devotee was seated beside her applying lotion to Mimi's legs and her softly bared stomach with slow, sensuously lingering hands. Mr. Jameson stared directly at Mimi's face, steadily and expressionlessly. He joggled his drink, finished it off. He turned to go, stopped and looked at her with transfixed eyes, as if rooted. It obviously took real effort to finally break away. . . . He'd never followed up; but Mimi knew he'd like to . . . given the occasion. The occasion was a costume ball.

"Mr. Jameson," Mimi told Randy, "hasn't made a proposition. He's looking for an opening. I haven't given him one. Tonight I will. Let me tell you what the girls say about him."

He nodded, watching her walk around the room, already in her costume as a Paris street rat. She was wearing a thin, breast revealing knit sweater, and a shiny black skirt that clung so tightly that the dimple in each buttock was visible as she moved. The side of the skirt was a slit above her hip.

At the upper point of the slit where her panties should have been there was nothing. Just bare flesh. She lifted her leg, resting a foot on the dressing table bench and strapped to her outer thigh a small, elegant knife. She lowered her leg, walked past the mirror, watching across her shoulder. Her leg moving across the slit showed the intriguing flash of the knife.

"Haven't you got any pants on?"

"No." She stopped, faced the mirror and put on the beret that went with the costume. She'd brushed her hair down to her eyebrows in sexy bangs, and darkened lids and lashes for a smoldering effect. Her mouth was a splash of sensual color. "No pants. Added intrigue. What the girls say is that he won't marry any of the older women he's been dating. Won't marry at all. He'll take a young mistress. Not only will but *should*."

She put a cigarette in her mouth, stood with one hip jutted sideward, her fist on it, her bare leg showing sexily in the slit. She looked at Randy sneeringly, snapped her fingers.

"Light," she commanded out of the corner of her mouth.

He frowned, hesitated.

"Oh, part of the costume?" He lit for her, nodding. "You do it well."

She exhaled smoke into his eyes and walked away.

"The girls go further. His mistress needn't be unmarried. Probably should be married. And someone in the community. Otherwise a glamor adventuress might yank him to the ends of the earth, disrupt his life and career. It would be better, more stable for him to have a discreet, happy affair right here at home. Cynical, but sensible."

"Are you proposing that YOU might be that mistress?"

She glanced at the clock, went over and lay down on the bed.

"Yes," she said. "Very discreet. Not crudely commercial. Immediate gifts or money would go with the wind. We'd be left with nothing. He can express his gratitude in a lasting, solid way. Giving you extra promotions, more responsibility. It would expand your field, give you a larger chance to make it. For you a lifetime career gain. For you and me both, bigger money, coming in surer, longer. . . . O.K."

"The whole idea's outrageous. It's time to go."

Driving to the club, Randy, looking like a middle-aged juvenile delinquent in cap, jersey and tight pants of a Paris tough, scowled and thought. When they parked Mimi said:

"In this costume, I could really turn it on Jameson tonight."

"Oh, he'd want you. But you put out free. Why would he pay off?"

She said nothing. She waited.

"On the other hand, if you got him wanting it bad enough. . . . And where's he going to do better? There's not a man in my division with a wife up to you in looks." There was an avaricious light in his eyes.

"O.K.," she said, getting out of the car. "I'll go to work on him."

She could be as bold and obvious as she pleased in the spirit of the costume. She went in and drew whistles and in response she sneered and flipped her hips and swaggered around, rolling her bottom. The knife on her thigh called attention to the bareness at the top of the slit.

She was the talk of the ball. She spotted Jameson in a wig and satin knee breeches and advanced on him, her stilt heels clacking out an aggressive rhythm. She grabbed him. "Hey, you, what're you got up for . . . a minuet? Come along!"

She towed him, laughing and delighted, out onto the floor. She clasped her hands around his neck and hung, dancing a vulgar burlesquey bump-grind-push-it-up. It came through howlingly funny. Along with the big joke he got the feel of the hot pressure and motion of her body.

"Kiss me, lover!" she demanded at the end of the dance and pulled him down by the ears and glued her mouth to his and began to dart her tongue rapidly, exciting him.

"That's all . . . you're discarded!" Mimi walked away flaunting her hips. She left him with remembered heat for an hour, meantime dancing with Jock in a Roman charioteer outfit.

When she started the game with Jameson a second time, he was right in there playing it hard.

"I like you, no joke," Mimi whispered.

Driving home Randy was enthusiastic, when she reported that she'd been propositioned and it was only a matter of setting time and place. Days later she reported she'd set up the first rendezvous. She left the house and drove around and came back and reported Jameson's passion in great detail. On the next occasion she said she'd put the proposition of Randy's advancement to him and he'd agreed.

It went on for weeks, months. Randy was building up to the day of the annual promotions with huge expectations. She occasionally dated other men when she was supposed to be with Jameson. Gradually, she centered back on Jock, who liked her company. A week before Randy's upcoming promotion Jock, who had no idea what she was up to, came to the house in the middle of the day, and insisted they go instantly to a motel.

He demonstrated to her his regained potency. While he was loving her he asked the ritual question. "Did you ever have so damned much fun in your life?" And she gave the ritual response. But her words were toneless. Afterward, she told him:

"No fun. Go marry your analyst."

147

"Don't be petty, sweetheart. I'm happy. Cured. Marry me."

"We'll see if you have a relapse. Meantime I'm getting other kicks."

"No possible relapse. We dug it out. . . . It came out, tearing my insides out. . . . But I found out why I feared marriage. It was infantile guilt. A terrible hidden fear of living in a home with a wife figure, wife-mother figure. As if loving such a symbol was incest. When I was five years old I was so possessive about my mother that I took a shotgun into her bedroom and wanted to murder both her and my father, while they were in each other's arms." He shuddered. "It was totally blanked out of conscious memory . . but unconsciously motivating me . . . you're not *interested?*"

"Like you were, Jock, I am now. Not capable of such intensities. . . . I'm going for the old kicks these days. We'll stay shallowed out."

The time of Randy's advancement in salary and position had come and gone.

He came home, raging. "I didn't even get the *usual* salary raise."

Mimi threw a convincing fit of outrage, then said calmly, "I'll fix him. But good. Really make him squirm and crawl. He'll retroactive it through. I'll invite him to dinner. . . . Yes, that's it. Leave it to me!"

The date was set. Jameson was glad to come. Mimi engaged extra help and the dinner was elegantly served on a table that gleamed and glowed with their best china, glassware, silver, flowers.

When they retired to the front room for liqueurs Mimi winked slyly at Randy. It had already been arranged that she should do the talking. She arrayed herself gracefully in a chair facing both of them from a point in a triangle. Her cream colored gown was expensive and gracefully loose, clinging like a mist to her supple body. The draping was cunning so that with her every breath the material clung to the points of her breasts and arranged itself in a pattern of shadowy furrows and ridges radiating outward from the nipples. Without staring Mr. Jameson politely enjoyed her and his liqueur and a cigar.

"Now," Mimi said sweetly, "I think we can all be frank

148

with one another at this stage. We're close enough friends for that!"

"By all means," Jameson agreed.

"Randy's a little angry with you. I can't blame him. We did believe your word was good."

Jameson set down his liqueur. He smiled uncomfortably.

"I don't quite understand."

"His raise and promotion! I don't like to say 'payment for value received' . . . but you *have* found my favors valuable in their own way." She lowered her lashes and smiled.

"Favors? What the hell is this?"

Randy had begun to stare and blink, his mouth open. He looked at her with a kind of emerging horror.

"You needn't be sly . . . Randy knows I've been sleeping with you twice and three times a week for months. The terms were understood. Agreed on by Randy and me, and you. Now, no nonsense, Mr. Jameson. I can get nasty mean and bitchy if you don't make good on the agreement!"

Jameson stared at her, at Randy. His face had drained. He finally said hoarsely:

"That was your understanding, Partch? That you would receive a promotion?"

"Of course it was," Mimi said for him. "Speak up, Randy, speak up. I'm not going to carry the ball all the way."

"Yes, That was the understanding."

"You'd *permit* your *wife* . . . to . . ." He broke off.

"I initiated it," Mimi said. "Don't imagine Randy dreamed up a plan like that."

"He did knowingly consent to—ah—our liaison. . . . You did, Partch. . . . Yes. . . . I see." Jameson got to his feet. "Where's my coat, please?" Mimi followed him to the entryway. So did Randy.

"We're having friends of yours in. . . . you said you'd stay, Mr. Jameson," she said sweetly.

He stared at her. "You're incredible, Mrs. Partch." He turned coldly to Randy. "Let me tell you, Partch, that there has *never* been *any* sexual liaison between me and your wife."

"You're. . . ." Randy worked his mouth like a landed

149

fish. "You're both lying! Aren't you?" he almost begged.

"No," Mimi said gaily. "It was all a joke, Randy. Just a game. My God, no, Mr. Jameson never so much as put a hand on me or even invited me to bed let alone taking me there. Can't you take a joke?"

"Well, Mrs. Partch, however detestable your scheme, it has succeeded. The fellow is destroyed in my eyes. There is nothing he can say to reinstate himself. Inform him to clear out his office." He left without acknowledging Randy still existed.

✣ SIXTEEN ✣

RANDY WANTED to hit her then, but their first guests arrived as Jameson drove off. Mimi was uniquely gay during the rest of the evening. Every time she caught Randy's eye from a safe distance behind a wall of guests she grinned tauntingly.

Finally, all the guests were gone and Randy, very drunk, followed her into her bedroom. She stood indifferently removing earrings, a gloating smile on her lips.

He took off his coat, saying in a strangulated voice: "I'm going to give you a beating!"

She laughed and fled for the bathroom, reaching out to slap his paunch in passing. He punched the air beside her head. She slammed into the bathroom and locked the door. He stormed around to the other door.

Mimi was beside it and tripped him when he rushed in. He fell flat on the tile. Mimi jeered and pushed him lightly with the toe of her shoe.

He got up in an apoplectic rage and started to chase her in dead earnest, his face burstingly red. Mimi skipped, hopped and danced, swinging chairs into his path and darting behind tables. He got close and swung one fist, then the oether, flailing like a windmill, his fury mounting each time he missed. He grazed her once and she went down, off balance. He jumped on her and smashed her in the face. She rolled, lurched her midsection, upsetting him and got up. She held her struck face and warned:

"That's enough!"

He wouldn't quit. Mimi flung her shoes at him and ran outside where his attack would be visible to neighbors. It didn't stop him. She ran to the back of the lot, then across.

She weaved and darted, outrunning him. He began to puff and she ran faster, around and around. She sprinted to the back of the lot, eyed the garage, then the house. He was puffing harder when he reached her. She set out at a straight, dead run. She reached the house yards ahead of him. She locked the door, rushed to get her car keys and purse. He smashed through a window and came at her, roaring with rage.

Mimi sprinted out of reach along the edge of the room. He dove at her, tackling her, bringing her down bruisingly. He started to crawl toward her head, his fists double, his lips drawn back viciously. In a frenzy Mimi began a wild torrent of blows, kneeing, kicking, hitting with her fists, clawing at his face, and trying to scoot away from him. He took all her blows and started a shattering blow toward her face. At the last instant Mimi rolled. He bellowed with pain and outrage.

She leaped to her feet, and as he came upward toward her, panting and furious, she seized a heavy table lamp and swung it overhead and down on his skull. He grunted and wobbled and started to go down. Then as he grabbed for her leg, catching and ripping her dress, she hit him with the lamp again.

When he got to his feet he was dull-eyed and staggering, his mouth open and panting. He swung futilely at her. She danced back, avoiding him easily. Then she stopped and glared. Ducking her head she ran at him, butting him so hard in the chest it knocked him off his feet onto his back.

She rushed to her bureau, wanting only to get out. She saw her leather driving gloves and put them on. He lay over there on his back, making half-conscious motions, trying to sit up. He got into a sitting position and stared in her direction. She rushed at him; struck him full in the face with her knee, then the other knee, knocking him on his back again.

She gave a sudden fierce cry and leaped on him, straddling his chest. She began to punch his face bloody. He swore and lurched, trying to throw her off. She buried the points of her knees in his arms, holding them helpless and rode him like a tigress, her fists battering his face. When he lifted his head she hammered it down.

When the protest went out of him, she just sat on his chest, watching his face for signs of returning conscious-

152

ness. He opened his raw eyes, quiveringly, and suddenly howled as she started to hit again. She skinned off one glove, put her knuckles to his mouth.

"Pucker," she demanded.

He swore. She bashed him five or six times and again presented her fist. He kissed it. Mimi got up and walked swaggeringly up and down beside him. He watched her anxiously.

"Get up," she commanded finally.

He stood. She knocked him onto the bed. He turned face down. She straddled his back and undid his pants, hauled them down, and removed the belt. When he tried to turn, she made a clawing gesture, threatening to rip his manhood. He lay there and took his beating. She lashed viciously, raising welts and drawing blood through his shorts.

When he merely begged for mercy she did not stop. Only when he lost control, when the pain became so unbearable that he screamed and sobbed did she quit. Stepping away, she was startled by a violent spasm of sexual excitement that suddenly flooded through her.

She clawed at her belly to stop the sensation and backstepped away from him in horror, her mouth open and panting. Her sexual thrill was rising inexorably toward an *orgasm.* A perverted, sadistic twisted ecstasy! She ran into the bathroom, locked herself in. She stood bracing her feet apart and got fistfuls of her own hair and yanked and yanked, causing herself eye-watering pain. Slowly, slowly the sexual feeling diminished, cooled.

She peeled off her ripped gown, went in her room, got a skirt, blouse and topcoat. Randy lay motionless just as she'd left him, except his eyes moved, following her venomously. Locked in the bathroom Mimi changed her clothes. She heard Randy moving.

In a minute there was a thunderous crash against the door, then another. He was battering it with a chair. When the door began to splinter, Mimi went out the window. She stopped in the kitchen, got a heavy butcher knife, then ran to the garage. She was starting her car when she saw him coming. She got out, went toward him, threatening him with the knife. He backed off, retreated to the house. Mimi slashed two tires of the other car, and went roaring out of the drive in her own.

153

She sped to the shack, stark-eyed, a black fright in her. Blessedly Jock was there! Good and well, and wholesomely clean and powerful enough with his love to carry her away from such sick, perverted joys.

He was on the steps, waiting, as she ran up, crying out to him. Inside, she stood shaking, her teeth chattering and barely able to speak. She began to gasp out what she had done. . . .

Before she had finished, Jock had her soothed, and they sat reclined on the bunk. Within an hour she was feeling safe.

"It's all right," Jock assured her. "You have no real capacity for perversion, sweetheart. From now on . . ."

That's when the sonic boom smashed the window. The glass shattered. Spots appeared on the opposite wall. They both leaped up. She looked at Jock, dumbstruck. He knew before she did that it wasn't a sonic boom.

The second shot came with a distinct roar, like a distillation of the roar of the sea. Then Randy was coming in, a long gun in his hand. Mimi saw the barrel of it spit yellow. A stripe of red like a claw mark appeared on Jock's cheek and temple. The line began to ooze blood. For a fraction he was like a top, stopping, tottering, spinning on its point, and then he was falling . . . falling.

Randy came at her, his bruised face puffed featureless, like some grisly monster, insane with pain, with rage and humiliation. He wagged the gun. He smiled murderously. Mimi began to retreat until she hit the wall. She opened her mouth and screamed.

"We are going to make love in special ways," Randy said harshly. "Then, I am not going to shoot you in the body. I'll begin with shooting off your toes, sweetheart. When you come to after you've fainted with pain," Jock, merely stunned, was stirring faintly there behind Randy, "next I'll aim at your kneecaps . . . and then, Mimi, while I am enjoying things. . . ." He stopped talking. He heard, or saw reflected somewhere, Jock moving, moving cautiously up from the floor.

Mimi could see Randy's finger curl around the trigger. He looked at her and said loudly: "Which can move fastest, Standish? Your whole body or my finger?"

While he was asking the question Jock's body was in

154

motion, catapulting like a released spring. One arm shot out ahead of his shoulder. His hand streaked upward, knocking the gun barrel up at a steep angle. The gun roared at the ceiling. A second later Jock had the gun. He swung it like a bat against Randy's head. He sprawled in a heap and lay still.

Jock went and called the police.

When the local police arrived Randy was still unconscious. At sight of him one of the cops drew a gun, pointed it at Jock. The other knelt by Randy, then phoned for an ambulance. Waiting, the police took their names, listened impassively to their stories. In a few minutes two State troopers arrived, listened just as bleakly to Jock's and Mimi's stories. The ambulance came. While the stretcher men carried Randy out the local police captain said nastily:

"Lover kills hubby."

"He's not dead," Jock pointed out. "As I told you, he broke in here and tried to kill us."

"I heard you, boy. What I see is a love nest and a half-dead hubby. C'mon, I'm booking the pair of you."

"On what charges? This is my home. Look there at the shot in the walls. Look at the pattern of broken glass. Anybody can see that a rifle was fired from outside. Check the gun and you'll find his fingerprints are on it. . . . mine are only on the barrel."

"Shut your mouth and don't learn me my job," he said, drawing his gun again, "and get down to my car. Moving slowly."

They put Mimi in a cell with a drunken woman. When, after an hour they took her out and questioned her again, there was a reporter and photographer there.

"This'll be a big one. The wires will pick it up. Swanky love nest slaying."

"He's not dead, is he?" Mimi flung up one hand to shield her face as the camera flashed.

They returned her to the cell in twenty minutes, wouldn't let her see Jock. About three in the morning she saw him; they brought her out to face a squad of reporters and photographers with Jock.

"Say nothing!" Jock advised her. "I demand for the eighth time to be allowed to call a lawyer. Partch isn't

155

dead. We're being held illegally. My home was invaded by a would-be killer; I have a case of attempted homicide against Partch."

They let Jock call a lawyer. Then they were put in cells again. An hour-and-a-half later they were brought out.

The lawyer, a friend of Jock's that Mimi knew, was there, beaming.

"You're free. He recovered. The cops've checked your story and he sure as hell did shoot your joint up, Jock. They're slapping attempted homicide on him."

"Let's get out of here," Jock said.

At the shack Mimi sat out on the deck close beside Jock, watching the pale horizon. She found herself staring compulsively for the first glimpse of the sun itself. She nestled against him.

"She used to say, my mother did, that it was never too late for a fresh new start. . . . Maybe while I'm getting my divorce in Nevada, I can get in touch with her. . . . it might not be too late for her either. . . . if she knows it's going to be so good for me. . . ."

She stopped talking. The sun appeared. That was their signal. They kissed lingeringly. Then Jock said silkily:

"I know something that's more damned fun than. . . ."

Mimi made a purring sound in her throat.

The End